SWIMMING
WITH
GHOSTS

The characters and events portrayed in this book are fictitious. Any similarity to real persons, living or dead, is coincidental and not intended by the author.

ISBN: 9781079225617

For my family,
who has taught me that art
comes in many forms,
including the written page

Chapter One

"There was blood everywhere. It was on the floor, on the walls, even on the ceiling."

"And that didn't freak you out?" asked Murphy.

"No, not really," replied Melissa.

"Mollie gets all light-headed when she gets a mosquito bite."

"I do not," she replied with a giggle.

"Tell them the truth," added Jeff.

"What do you mean?"

"Not only did it *not* freak her out, it turned her on, like an aphrodisiac."

"Oh, stop. It did not. I was a little excited, though," she continued, after a short pause.

"Excited over a crime scene? You're a strange bird."

"I was thrilled because it was my first assignment outside of the lab. They brought me there to take pictures to try to determine what happened. That's what I went to school for. And now, here I was, investigating my first murder. Me! Not only collecting evidence, but making contributions to help solve the crime."

"Did you?"

"Did I what?"

"Solve the crime?"

"Oh, hell yes. He didn't stand a chance. He was a slob.

He tried to clean things up, but to be honest, he made it so freaking easy for us. His finger prints were everywhere. Once we had the prints and got a hit in the database, he was apprehended in less than forty-eight hours."

"What database are you referring to?"

"IAFIS. It stands for Integrated Automated Fingerprint Identification System. It's maintained by the FBI and includes prints submitted by local, state and federal law enforcement agencies throughout the country. The dude had a record, so his prints were on file."

"That's unbelievable."

"That was my first job. I wasn't sure if I had the stomach for it, but it turned out that I did. And I've been doing it ever since."

"Murphy's first job was pretty memorable, too," responded Mollie.

"Oh, jeez, did you have to bring that up?"

"Come on… we're talking about first jobs. Tell them."

"Yeah, tell us," replied Melissa.

"Fine. It was something like fifteen or twenty years ago. I was in sales."

"You've always been in sales, haven't you?" asked Jeff.

"That's where the money is. I'm fresh out of school and I got a gig selling life insurance for a small insurance company."

"This is so funny," added Mollie. "I laugh every time he tells this."

"So, they give me this envelope one day and ask me to drop it off to an address on the way home."

"What was it?"

"Oh, I had no idea. I figured it was a recent policy that got approved, and since it was on my way home, I could just hand deliver it, you know trying to exceed service expectations. I knew it was weird right from the beginning, because it wasn't for one of my customers. But, whatever. So, I get to the house, and there are cars everywhere. I have no idea what's going on, so I knock on the door. Some guy lets me in, and I see that the place is swarmed with people."

"A party?"

"Nope. A fucking funeral. The place was filled with family and friends, and everyone was in mourning."

"No!"

"Yep."

"They never told you?"

"That would have been a good nugget of information to have, wouldn't it? No, they didn't. So, I go in the house and I ask around for the name on the envelope and it turns out it was her."

"Who?"

"The widow. That's when it dawned on me... I was hand-delivering a death benefit check. That's when I freaked out."

"What do you mean?"

"I ran straight to the bathroom and threw up. Of course, I tripped over an end table on the way and knocked over a couple of drinks."

"Oh my God, are you serious?"

"I couldn't do it. I couldn't look her in the eyes. I was totally caught off-guard. It was way too emotional."

"Let me get this straight. You had one job to do, you walked into her house, knocked over some furniture and then threw up."

"Yeah, that's pretty much how it went down. After that, I practically collapsed."

"I think you did," replied Mollie.

"No, but I came close. I got really lightheaded and had to sit down for a while."

"But you gave her the check?"

"Of course. That's why I was there, apparently. But as soon as I got back to the office, I quit."

"Why? Because they didn't warn you in advance?"

"Look, I understand what life insurance is for. And I'm certain that was the exact reason the family took it out. But my job is to sell that security... that piece of mind. Never in a million years did I think they would ask me to deliver the check. Maybe some people like to feel like the hero. But nobody prepares you for that type of emotion. I just... that was it. It was my first and my last. I'll sell it all day long, but if my role included swimming in those emotional pools every day, well... I just couldn't see myself doing it without being affected."

"That's a crazy story."

"That was one of my first jobs, and quite honestly, my shortest."

"Speaking of pools... your new pool looks gorgeous!"

Mollie and Murphy were hosting a barbecue for their best friends, Jeff and Melissa, who had just moved into town. Medium-rare filets, grilled garlic asparagus, and bottomless glasses of Merlot contributed to an evening full of love and laughter.

"Thank you. Truthfully, it was never on our radar," said Murphy. "But I had a dream."

"Go on, Martin Luther King."

"No, seriously. It was strange, it felt so real. I was grilling after work. Mollie was floating around the pool in one of those inflatable lounge chairs. We had dinner and chilled in and out of the pool all night long. It was so relaxing. I woke up and felt so refreshed, like I could conquer the world. We talked about it for quite a while, and decided to pull the trigger."

"They did a great job. How long did it take?"

"Three months."

"When did they finish?"

"Two weeks ago."

"Well, enjoy. It's a great way to decompress after work each day," added Jeff.

"Aren't you afraid of raising a child around a pool?" asked Melissa.

"Nah. That's why they have safety gates. Plus, there are plenty of great learn-to-swim programs for infants in the area. It's amazing how young some of them are when they're first introduced to water instruction. Besides... that's down the road."

"Down the road? No baby plans yet?" inquired Melissa.

"Oh, we have plans," interrupted Mollie. "It's just taking some time."

"But you guys are trying?"

"Every chance we get," replied Murphy. "We've had sex there, and there, and there, and there..." he said, as he began pointing around different areas of the home. "But enough about our sex life. Have you guys gotten settled in yet?"

"You mean, have we unpacked the thousand boxes we moved here with?"

"That's it? Just a thousand?" joked Murphy.

"It's a staggering task, isn't it?" replied Mollie. "We were tripping over boxes for weeks when we moved."

"Yeah. It's still a work-in-progress. But we're getting there."

"How's the job at the new crime lab working out, Mel? Any different than the old one?" asked Murphy.

"I love it. And this one has some great, new equipment for me to play with. Some people think it's boring work, and to be honest, it can be. Sometimes it takes days, even longer, to lift prints and scour evidence for DNA. But it's so rewarding when the work you do can assist law enforcement in the world of justice," replied Melissa.

"I'll bet that's interesting work," commented Mollie as she poured another glass of wine for her guests.

"You have no idea. I can't go into too many details, but we're working on identifying someone involved in a string of local burglaries."

"Right here? In our own backyard?"

"You're glad I moved into the area, aren't you? Just trying to make the neighborhood a safer place."

"Well, thank you. I feel better knowing that you're on the job."

"Thank you. But enough about my job, as exciting as it is. I heard you're starting a new one, too!"

"Yeah," replied Murphy. "Same company I'm with right now, but I got a promotion. I start in my new role next week."

"You were a broker, right?"

"Yeah. But I just got promoted to Sales Manager."

"That's fantastic! Congratulations!"

"Thank you. I'm really excited. A little nervous, but thrilled at the prospect of almost doubling my salary."

"Wow! That's a heck of a bump!"

"Well, kind of. My salary went up a little, but I now get to work on bigger accounts. They're harder to close, but when I do, the commissions should eclipse those I earned in my previous role."

"Well, cheers to new beginnings," said Jeff, as he raised his glass in celebration.

"Amen," replied Murphy, as they all clinked their glasses.

Chapter Two

"Stand still," said Mollie. "I can't tie this with you fidgeting around like that."

"Sorry. I guess I have the first day jitters," replied Murphy.

"Tell me again why you have to wear this silly bow tie on your first day?"

"It's not silly! It's my lucky tie!"

"You don't need luck. You already have the job."

"I know. But it's a classy tie."

"Which you don't know how to tie, Mr. Master's Degree from Stanford."

"But it makes a great first impression."

"Who are you trying to impress?" she asked, as she untied the tie to try again, for the fourth time.

"I've been assigned a mentor. He's one of the Vice Presidents of the firm."

"What's his name."

"Joe."

"How long has he been there?"

"Gosh, I don't know. Longer than me. He's pretty successful, too. I'm going to be shadowing and working on and off with him for the next six months. Word on the street is he's being groomed for President of Sales down the road. My new role has the potential to replace him if

8

he gets it."

"Really? I didn't know that."

"Well, let me rephrase that. The Sales Manager role is used as a development opportunity. But it's typically to develop a pipeline of future candidates for higher positions."

"So, if you do well...?"

"The sky's the limit. Who knows... if I do well, I mean really well... It's quite possible I might get fast-tracked to my next position. Not that I'm in a rush, don't get me wrong. But there's a lot of movement within the company."

"That's very encouraging. Is this Joe person a nice guy?"

"Honestly, I don't really know him. I mean, I know *of* him. His name has always been at the top of the sales sheets."

"Well so has yours, baby," she replied, as she finally finished with his tie. "There you go. All set. You look very dapper."

Murphy turned to look at her handiwork in the mirror. "Nice. It looks great. Thank you."

"One day you'll have to learn how to do this yourself."

"I could probably never do it as good as you," he responded, as he gave her a gentle kiss on the cheek. "Besides, it's my tradition that I only wear this on my first day. Every other day is a regular tie."

"I have no doubt you'll be able to celebrate many more first days in the future," replied Mollie, as she brushed a piece of lint from his left sleeve. "Before you know it, you'll be running the place."

"I appreciate the confidence. Let's see if I can pull this gig off, first."

"You look great. Knock 'em dead, lover."

"Thanks. I'll call you later."

"You better. And remember, I'm ovulating today. So, you know what we're doing tonight."

"In that case, I'll be home early," he replied with a smile.

Chapter Three

"I'm sure I don't need to remind you, but I'll say it anyway. This is not a nine-to-five job."

Joe was holding an introductory meeting with three newly promoted employees in the Sales Manager position. In their previous incarnation, they were brokers, and productive ones, at that. It was the next step in a well-defined career path at Sterling Investments. Of course, success in a prior role didn't guarantee success in a new one. The stakes were larger, the hours were longer, and the pressure, well... the pressure to sell was never-ending. But the financial carrot that was dangling in front of them was the motivator. For anyone pursuing a career path in sales, it's all about the money.

"You need time off for personal things, take time off. I'm not going to manage your calendar. The bottom line is results. This is a sales position, and Sterling Investments expects results. I don't care if it takes forty hours a week or eighty hours a week. All I care about is results. Next... all deals go through me. No exceptions. Whether it's something you generated organically or something we developed as a team. You're all good at what you do. That's why you're here. My job is to make you better. Your homework assignment today is to work on your elevator speech."

"What's that?" asked one of the managers.

"If you were riding on an elevator with someone, what could you say in thirty seconds that says who you are, who you represent, and what you can do for them. I'm not asking you to figure out how to close a deal in that short timeframe. But at the end, you want that person not only interested in you and what you have to offer, but also hungry for more. We'll meet back at 3pm and you can pitch me what you've each come up with. That's all. Get to work and let's start generating some leads."

The three managers all got up to depart.

"Murphy, hang back for a minute, please."

"Sure…"

Joe started typing some random keys on his keyboard but clearly wasn't successful at whatever he was attempting. He wanted to show Murphy something on his computer, but couldn't get past the login screen. "Dammit. I hate this thing. Give me one second. Amy! Aaaaaay-Meeeeee!"

"You don't have to shout," she replied, as she rounded the corner and entered his office. "I'm literally right outside your office."

"You weren't answering me."

"I was on the phone. Your phone."

"Oh, sorry to interrupt. But I need help."

"Tell me something I don't know," she replied sarcastically. "What's the problem this time?"

"I can't get logged in. This computer is a piece of shit."

"The computer's fine. It's probably something you did. Are you getting some type of error message?"

"Yeah, it says my login ID isn't recognized. I'm using the same freaking username I use every day."

"Maybe your fat fingers typed it in wrong."

Joe stared at her with a strange look that said something to the effect of "Seriously? You think I would make that kind of mistake?"

"Let's try again. Let me see the exact message."

"I'm sure I typed it in correctly. God, I hate these things," he replied, as he tapped away on the keyboard.

"Well, look at that. You're in," she said.

"I swear I typed the exact same thing last time."

"Maybe I just needed to stand over your shoulders. I give off a special aura."

"Amy's aura," commented Murphy.

"Amy's aura," she repeated. "I like that. I should figure out a way to bottle that stuff up and sell it. I'd make a fortune."

Joe interrupted their banal banter. It was way more than he cared to hear that early in the morning. "Goodbye, Amy."

Amy smiled and commented to Murphy on her way out. "Personally, I think his computer is possessed by a ghost, and its sole purpose is to irritate him."

"You two seem to have an interesting relationship," said Murphy, once Amy was out of the room.

Joe leaned his head over to ensure she was back at her desk and out of earshot. "She's a great gal. We had a thing one time. Our personalities just meshed."

"She's got a 5-year anniversary magnet on her file cabinet. Haven't you been married longer than that?"

"Look at you, Mr. CSI. Yes, but if you must know, the wife and I went through a rough patch and took a break. She helped me get through it."

"I'll bet she did," he said sarcastically.

"It's not like that. Well, it was, sort of," he smirked.

"She was a good friend. But that's in the past. Now it's all work and no play. What about you? Any extra-curricular activities on the marriage front? Be honest."

"Me? No... Mollie and I are like peanut butter and jelly. We go together."

"That's cute. You never looked to see if the grass was greener on the other side?"

"Nope. The thought never crossed my mind."

"Good for you," said Joe. "A strong marital foundation can definitely play a role in your success in this position. I learned that the hard way. My third wife is definitely a keeper."

"I'm glad you finally found what you were looking for."

"Me too," Joe replied, as he punched some keys on the keyboard.

Murphy continued to glance around the room and noticed a number of awards and accolades dispersed throughout. "That's a pretty fancy award on your desk."

"This? It's just another gimcrack I got for blowing out my quota."

"Gimcrack?"

"Yeah... you've never heard that term before?"

"No."

"It's one of those fancy SAT words. It's just a cheap and showy ornament. You know, a tchotchke." Joe continued to pound away on his keyboard and spun around his monitor. "This is our focus for the upcoming presentation."

Murphy read the screen out loud. "401k Management Plans."

"Have you ever sold any?"

"Nope."

14

"These are exciting, because you're not selling mutual funds or annuities to a single person. You're selling the concept of retirement investing to a group, and some of them can be pretty large. And the benefit to that is…?"

"More investors, bigger commissions."

"Exactly. A lot of small employers have steered clear of offering 401k plans to their employees for a number of reasons. The biggest concerns are that they think they're complicated to establish and costly to administer. That's where we come in. We're a full-service firm. We take the guess work out of it, and our fees are incredibly competitive with others in the marketplace. We help make the task easier. We not only offer affordable plans, we also act as administrators and investment counselors. We relieve them of the complexities of investing, and allow their employees to put retirement saving on cruise control."

"Sounds like you just wrote my elevator speech for me," he chuckled.

"Ha ha. So, here's your homework assignment. I need you to read up on all of our available plans. We have a presentation coming up for a small company, and Sterling wants you in on the gig."

"How small?"

"About thirty employees. They tried managing investment options themselves, but it quickly became overwhelming and expensive. That's our cue. We pitch the plan, roll over their accounts, and in less than sixty days we add almost two million dollars in investment funds to our portfolio."

"That's a big number."

"Welcome to the big leagues, brother. This is the game we play."

15

Chapter Four

Knock knock!
"Hi. You must be Mollie."
   "I am," she answered. "And you are…?"
   "I'm Joe. From the firm. I work with your husband."
   "Oh, Joe. Right. Murphy has told me so much about you. Please, come in."
   "Thank you," he replied, as he took off his shoes in an effort to not to track any dirt on their beautiful hardwood floors.
   "Murphy! You have company."
   "Hey Joe. This is a surprise. Is everything okay?"
   "Hi Murph. Sorry for stopping by unannounced. I just wanted to drop off some paperwork and other items for the trip tomorrow. I wanted to make sure you had all the brochures and other literature we talked about."
   "Thanks. Come in for a bit."
   "Joe," began Mollie, who shifted into hostess mode, "can I get you anything? Coffee, soda, water?"
   "Water would be great. Thank you."
   Mollie departed for the kitchen, leaving the two of them to talk.
   "She seems very sweet."
   "Love of my life," Murphy replied.
   "How long have you two been married?"

"Seven years."

"Is it just the two of you? This is a pretty big house."

"A family is in our future. It's just taken a little more time than we thought."

Mollie returned with his water and the three sat down to chat.

"Hey, I'm glad you're here," said Murphy. "I had a couple of questions on one of our funds, I was hoping you might be able to offer some clarification."

"What's the question?"

"Hold on, one sec. Let me go grab my binder."

Murphy retreated to his study, leaving Mollie and Joe alone in the living room.

"So, Mollie. What's the 4-1-1 on Murphy?"

"The 4-1-1?"

"Yeah. The info. The skinny. The inside scoop. We have a new relationship and I don't know much about him. I was hoping maybe you could accelerate my knowledge."

"What would you like to know?"

"Whatever you can tell me in the next minute while he's out of the room. What kind of food does he like? What does he like to drink? What kind of music does he listen to? What's his middle name?"

Mollie answered each of the questions in succession, like she was competing on a game show. Murphy returned with some folders and a short list of items for which he needed clarification.

"This is where I leave, when the conversation turns to things I don't understand. Joe, it was a pleasure meeting you."

"The pleasure's mine, Mollie. Enjoy your evening. I promise I won't take too much of his time."

"Thank you."

Chapter Five

Two days later, Joe and Murphy were on the road. They travelled to their destination in the afternoon, intent on getting a good night's rest at the hotel before their presentation the next morning.

Knock knock!

"Hey! Are you in there? We're gonna be late!"

Joe stood there with his ear pressed to the door, listening for any sign of movement from the room within.

"Come on, man! I can hear you snoring! Wake up, you loser!"

His knocks became louder as he started pounding on the door. *Bam! Bam! Bam!*

He heard a faint "I'm up," followed by footsteps, and finally the unlocking of the hotel door.

"I'm up. Stop making a big ruckus," Murphy stated, as he opened the door.

"Not a good way to make a first impression, brother. You know how important today is. I can't believe you overslept."

"Did I?" he answered groggily, as he turned around and approached the cheap five-dollar alarm clock supplied by the hotel chain. He picked it up and held it close to his face, as his eyes were having trouble focusing. "Holy shit! It's 7:30? We're going to be late!"

"Welcome to the party, Mr. Let's-Just-Have-One-More-Whiskey-Before-Bed. Glad we're finally on the same page."

"Ten minutes," he replied. "That's all I need."

"That's all you get. If you're not downstairs in ten minutes, I'm leaving without you."

"Ten minutes. I promise."

"Fine. I'll be in the lobby."

This was a big day for Murphy. His first presentation in the presence of his new boss. Okay, so he got off to a rough start. Alcohol often puts him into a deep sleep, making him groggy the next morning. But he knew how important the day was, and had full confidence he could pull it off. He would not fail in the eyes of his employer.

Upon exiting the shower, he began to mentally prepare. Joe had mentioned it was a two-million-dollar account. The reality was, in the 401K corporate arena, this wasn't necessarily a huge client. But the key in the investment world is an increasing investment base. They collected one percent of assets managed. As the assets grew and the employees saved more, their management fee grew. And if the company became more successful, they could potentially add more employees to manage. The key was to not only close the deal, but to get them to commit to a multi-year contract, providing recurring revenue to their own firm. Murphy was confident in his abilities. He knew what he had to do, and looked forward to getting in front of the client.

Chapter Six

The presentation went as well as he had hoped. It was a long drive home, but he always felt better sleeping in his own bed.

Murphy snuck out of bed in the middle of the night for a drink. It was just after 2am. It's strange the routine his body follows. He pulled a water bottle from the refrigerator and looked out the kitchen window. Much to his surprise, he saw a couple of random bubbles rise up from the pool. It lasted only about ten seconds, then stopped.

"What the f… That was weird," he thought to himself. He retired back into the bedroom and snuck back into bed quietly, so as not to wake his bride.

Later that morning, his wife was the first to awaken, and started the day as she always does, by making a pot of French Vanilla coffee, with some cinnamon sprinkled into the grinds for some extra flavor, and a pinch of salt to allay the bitterness.

"Good morning, Sunshine. Welcome to Tuesday," she said, as she greeted Murphy upon his arrival to the new day. "Sleep well?"

"Yeah. Hey, I need you to do me a favor when I'm at work today."

"Anything."

"Could you please call the pool contractor? I think we have a leak."

"A leak? It's brand new."

"I know. But I came out here last night for a drink, and I could swear I saw some bubbles rise to the surface."

"Maybe it was air working its way through the filter system?"

"Maybe, but it's under warranty, so let's have them come out and check."

"Okay. I'll call them. What do you have planned for work today?"

"Same as every other day. Lots of emails and cold calls, trying to generate more leads. A sales job is never done. We get accolades for all of the business we bring in, but the minute a new fiscal quarter starts, the pressure begins all over again."

"When is your next trip?"

"In two days. But it's a quick overnighter. We leave Thursday morning and return Friday afternoon."

"Okay, well good luck today," she said, as she turned to begin making a homemade breakfast.

Murphy spent most of the day as he normally does... generating new business. Some don't have the discipline for a career in sales. It was really nothing more than simple math. Make enough contacts and eventually someone will be interested. It was all about the activity. Contacts generate leads, and leads generate sales. Every day was filled with random phone calls and emails. His lead rate was running in the neighborhood of three percent, meaning every hundred contacts generated three leads, which he would then cultivate into a formal presentation. Typically, he would close one out of every nine leads, equating to a close rate of approximately eleven percent to the leads, and 0.3 percent to the contacts. It sounded more complicated than it was, but in the end, it was just math. If he wanted to close two deals a month, he just increased his contact count to six hundred. That broke down to one-hundred and fifty per week, or thirty a day, an easily manageable number. He was in the middle of his email brigade when Joe passed by his office and popped his head in.

"Congratulations, rookie!"

"It closed?" he asked.

"It did! Great job yesterday. We're still in paperwork mode, but they're on board. They signed a commitment, so it's as good as done. Sterling is pleased, especially since this was your first gig with the new product line. Whatever you decide to do tonight, make sure you celebrate!"

"Thanks, Joe! That's great news."

Joe departed and Murphy decided to share the news with his wife.

"Hey hon."

"Hey sweetie."

"Guess what?"

"You know I'm not good at this game."

"Then I'll spare you the suspense. The deal closed."

"The one from yesterday?"

"That's the one."

"The one that you were all nervous about?"

"Apparently we killed it during the presentation. They signed less than twenty-four hours later."

"Aww, that's amazing. Congratulations. We should celebrate tonight."

"And that, we will. Oh, by the way... Did you get a chance to call the contractor?"

"I did. They actually came out with a leak detection company, and they found nothing. The pool is fine."

"That's so weird."

"No, what's weird was the whole leak detection process. This guy puts on a set of headphones and runs a pole with a microphone through every wall and seal in the pool. He was quite thorough, but he looked like some dude with a metal detector on the beach."

"But he said the pool was fine?"

"Yep. All systems are a go."

"Okay, well, thank you for setting that up. I just... that was a pretty pricy project. This is the type of stuff that keeps me up at night."

"It's all good. Maybe you can grill tonight and we can float in the pool afterwards."

"That sounds like a perfect way to celebrate. Oh, and you should wear that two-piece bikini with the leopard print."

"You like that one, huh?"

"It's my favorite."

Chapter Seven

Murphy and Joe had a long day ahead of them. They were on the road for a presentation in Tallahassee. It was planned as a hit and run... in and out in one day. It was normally a four-and-a-half-hour drive from Tampa, but Joe had a bit of a lead foot, so it would likely be a tad shorter. The presentation wasn't scheduled until the afternoon, so they had plenty of time. Their travels took them up US 19, one road, straight into Tallahassee. It was a direct route with very little traffic once they got past the Weeki Wachee area. However, it did go through a number of small towns, forcing them to reduce their speed limit constantly, which frustrated Joe. "Dammit" was the most commonly used word that day.

They were on a stretch of road with little traffic when they saw a broken-down vehicle on the side of the road.

"We should stop and help," said Murphy.

"I don't think so," answered Joe. "We have places we need to be."

"We have plenty of time."

"Which we'll be using to make sure we're fully prepared."

"But the road is empty. There are no other cars for miles."

"That's why they have auto clubs. For situations such

as this."

"What if she's not a member?"

"I can't help it if she's stupid. That's her problem."

"You're a real warm and fuzzy kind of guy, aren't you?"

"Time is money, Murph. You all set for your part of the gig? You know all the funds and expense fees?"

"Yeah," he replied, as he looked in the mirror on his visor at the stranded vehicle they just passed.

"Good. We need to close this one. We can't exude confidence if you're up there fumbling with the facts."

"It won't be a problem, Joe. I got this."

"Look at this," Joe replied. "Another idiot. There's like, nobody on the road, yet here he is in the left lane. Left lane is for slower traffic, you donut-head," he shouted, as he passed him in the right lane.

Murphy was entertained by his partner's road rage. He was surprised that he was irritated as often as he was, seeing how he spent so much time on the road.

"Do you like driving?" asked Murphy.

"Me? Sure. Why do you ask?"

"It seems you get frustrated often."

"I can't help that there are so many people on the road who don't know how to drive. The reality is, it gets me out of the office. That place can get chaotic at times, and the road can sometimes be peaceful. Oh, hey, that sign coming up says we're thirty miles from Tallahassee. That'll put us in town about an hour before the first gig. Want to grab a quick bite for breakfast before we have to set up? My treat."

"Sure."

###

As anticipated, the presentation went smoothly. The organization already had their employee retirement accounts set up and managed by another financial firm. That firm, however, was being swallowed up and assets merged with another firm, which had an entirely different fee structure. This was their opportunity to shop around and see if there were other players on the landscape who could satisfy their needs without raising costs. This one was all about price.

"Do me a favor," said Joe, as they began their drive back to Tampa.

"Sure. What do you need?"

"Make a note to crunch some numbers when we get back. I saw it in their faces. Our rate was lower, but it might not be low enough for them to make the switch."

"What are you thinking?"

"I don't know. I want to forecast our revenue each year for the next five years. Specifically, I want to see what we would make if we waived the setup fee and discounted the management fees."

"You would do that?"

"Whatever it takes to make the sale. Just so you know, when you're out on your own, you have that authority."

"Good to know."

"Yeah, so just make some type of note to forecast our revenues if we dropped a quarter-point on the fees."

Murphy pulled out his phone and scrolled through the available applications, and activated one entitled 'Notes.' He pressed the microphone and began speaking into his phone to record Joe's comments. "When we get back, put the employee counts and current balances into a spreadsheet to forecast our..."

"Oh, come on, you freaking moron!" Joe shouted,

interrupting Murphy's audio note, forcing him to stop recording.

"Sorry… it's just…. The light's green and the dude's just sitting there. Sorry. I'll be quiet."

Murphy hit record again and began talking into his phone a second time. "Forecast what our revenues would be if we were to discount the…"

"Really? You're going to get in front of me in the left lane and then slow down? What a jerk!"

"Are you serious?" asked Murphy.

"What?"

"You can't drive thirty seconds without yelling at someone."

"Sure, I can. I'll stop. I promise. You can record your note."

"I'm good. I have enough of a note to know what I have to do. I'll circle back with you in the morning with the projections."

"Excellent. Then we can decide if the discount is feasible, or if it erodes our position too much."

There were a few minutes of silence in the car, until Murphy hit the 'play' button on his phone and replayed his two partial notes with Joe's road rage interruptions. The two of them laughed almost the entire trip home.

Chapter Eight

Later that night.

Mollie rolled over and flopped her hand on the opposite side of the bed. It was the middle of the night, but she quickly noticed something was amiss. The king-sized bed had more empty space than normal, as she noticed her husband wasn't in bed with her. She sat up, looked around, and focused her eyes on the LED glare of the time on the cable box. 2:30am. She pulled the covers off and got out of bed, in search for her spouse. Upon entering the kitchen, she ran into the love of her life, her high school sweetheart, drinking a glass of water.

"Are you okay?" she asked.

"Yeah, I'm fine," he replied, as he stood motionless staring outside the kitchen window.

"Are you having trouble sleeping?"

"No. just thirsty."

She stood next to him and began to rub his back.

"But there's an issue," he added.

"With what? It's not the pool, is it?"

He paused before answering. "The watermelons... They're not ripe enough to go surfing."

"What?"

"And if I take the leftover meatloaf to work, how will the dogs play tennis?"

His wife smirked. His gibberish made perfect sense… sort of. He was sleepwalking, which happened from time-to-time when he was stressed and his brain went on overload. It was his body's way of releasing that stress. His nonsensical statements were a byproduct of his unconsciousness. She had seen it before, so she was not alarmed.

"The tennis match is over, honey," she replied. "The dogs ate the meatloaf and went surfing instead, so you can take the watermelons to work."

He turned his head and faced her. A normal response to a comment such as that would be "what the hell are you talking about?" But in his current state, he just replied, "Really?"

"Yes. They should be ripe by the morning."

It didn't really matter what she said. Not only would his brain not fully process her comments, he wouldn't remember them in the morning, either.

"Oh… okay," he answered.

"Are you ready to come back to bed?"

He took one last sip of water and nodded his head. And with that strange, middle-of-the-night banter, she grabbed his hand and they departed into the bedroom, for the second time that evening.

Chapter Nine

"You walked again last night."

"Did I really?"

"Yeah. I thought you just went in for a glass of water, but when I spoke to you, I knew you were still asleep."

"Uh oh. What did I say? I didn't share missile codes with you, did I?"

"No, no missile codes," she chuckled. "But you did mention something about watermelons and surfing. It was cute, actually."

"Watermelons and surfing? One day you should try to record me. I'd love to hear the conversation."

"Sometimes you say the funniest things."

"I have absolutely no recollection of that."

"I thought about waking you, but figured the best approach was to just get you back into bed."

"I appreciate that. I can use all the rest I can get."

"Is everything going okay at work?"

"Me? Yeah. It's fine. Going great, actually."

"Okay. Just checking."

"Are you concerned I'm in over my head?"

"No... it's just... well, it's been a while since you walked in your sleep. It just took me by surprise."

"I'm sure it was just a random episode."

Mollie smiled. "You're right. I'm sure it was." Inside

her head, she was thinking, "I hope so."

Chapter Ten

"This seems like a nice place."

Murphy and Joe were traveling once again, this time for a few meetings just outside of Nashville. It was a quick, two-day trip, and they ended their day on the road as they usually do... at a bar that was typically picked at random.

"It'll work," replied Joe. "Listen, regarding tomorrow's presentation..."

"What about it?"

"I'd like you to play the lead."

"Are you sure? You gave the team that big speech, you know, all gigs run through you, etcetera."

"And I meant it. But we're going to be working quite a bit together, and I'd like to learn a little about your approach. Make no mistake... I'll be there, in the background. I'll be your copilot if you need me. But I'd like to get a sense of your style."

"My style?"

"Yeah. What you say, how you say it, how you answer questions and overcome objections. That sort of thing."

"That's fine."

"Me watching over your shoulder won't make you nervous?"

"No," laughed Murphy. "Should it?"

"I'm just asking. Most people get a little edgy when I'm around."

"Well, you are a little on the intimidating side, if I can be honest."

"Do you think that's a bad thing?"

"Me? No. In fact, I think there could be a certain synergy in teaming up, you know representing different presentation styles. You never know what's going to connect with the different people in the audience."

Joe turned his head and looked around the bar. "Where are all the women?"

"You're married."

"Yeah, yeah, yeah."

"It's early. I'm sure this place will fill up as the night goes on."

"No, seriously. All I see are guys."

"Feeling a little homophobic?"

"No, but... Holy Shit!"

"What?"

"That guy over there is holding hands with that other guy."

"So? You make it sound like it's a rare thing. It's 2019, Joe."

Joe continued to look around and carefully checked out every patron, until he caught eye contact with a gargantuan of a man, adorned with tattoos and leather. "Okay, stay calm."

Murphy took a sip of his drink. "I think you're overreacting."

"I'm pretty sure we're in a gay bar."

"Okay. Rookie mistake, but we are in a strange town. We just picked this place at random. It's not outside of the realm of possibilities. We'll finish our drink and then leave. It's not a big deal."

"Fuck! Yes, it is! That dude just winked at me!"

"Which one?" asked Murphy.

"Don't turn around. Oh my God, we need an exit strategy."

Just then, the immense stranger at the end of the bar turned and started walking towards them.

"Murphy, I'm your boss."

"Yeah."

"I need you to do something, no questions asked."

"Okay."

"Seriously, man. Blind obedience."

"I'm your guy. Team player, through and through."

"Kiss me," he whispered.

"What?"

"Kiss me!"

"Oh, I don't think so. I'm not gay."

"Neither am I, you moron. But I'm about to be hit on by the captain of the prison football team. He needs to know I'm here with you."

"You are here with me."

"You're not getting it. He needs to know I'm here *with* you."

"I'm not going to kiss you."

"Kiss me. And it's gotta look real. Now! He's almost here!"

"Joe, you have to chill..." And before Murphy could finish his sentence, Joe grabbed the sides of his head, pulled him close, and planted a big kiss right on his lips.

"Don't... fucking... move..." he gritted through his teeth.

Murphy was frozen. To say he was taken aback was an understatement. Seeing that the unimaginable was already in progress, he let his boss have his moment for about two to three seconds, though it likely felt like an eternity.

The large man approached as their lips pulled apart, and offered a simple "Hey guys" as he passed them on his way to the bathroom.

"Hey," Joe responded, as calmly as possible.

"I think it worked," said Murphy.

"Good. Come on, let's go."

"But I'm not done with my drink yet."

"Oh, yes you are. Come on," he repeated, as he grabbed his travel partner by the hand and made tracks for the exit.

"You know…" started Murphy in a sarcastic tone, "I really think you owe me dinner. I mean, I'm normally not this easy."

"Not a word of this to anyone. You hear me?"

"Got it," he laughed.

"Seriously. Not a soul. I would never hear the end of it."

"Not even Amy?" he asked, jokingly.

"Especially Amy!"

Chapter Eleven

Midnight, Thursday night.

Mollie heard the sound of a key in the door. She wasn't alarmed, as she was anticipating the return of her husband, although not this late in the evening.

"I'm home!" he said, as he entered the house.

"Hey, baby," she replied, as she gave him a big hug. "Welcome back. You're home late."

"Yeah, flight was delayed an hour. Then an hour and a half. Then two hours. Thanks for waiting up."

"You're welcome. I didn't want to end my day without seeing you. Was it a good trip?"

"It was. It was a great trip. Do you mind if I fill you in on the details tomorrow? I'm exhausted and ready to pass out."

"Of course. I'm ready for bed, too. I'm glad you're home safe…"

The two departed for the bedroom. Mollie quickly fell asleep and began to snore. Her snoring wasn't loud. It was like a tiny little buzz-saw. But it was enough to keep him up and prevent him from falling asleep. Murphy's brain, unfortunately, was still overloaded from the business trip, even though he was physically drained. He got up, as he frequently does, to get a drink. Maybe a little hydration would help. He glanced at the clock on the microwave.

2:14am. He then looked out of his kitchen window to stare at his gorgeous pool, one now he knows has no leak. And then... a bubble.

"Fuck me. Are you serious?"

The sporadic bubbles began to multiply, until it appeared as if that small section of the pool was filled with boiling water. Murphy was confused, scared, angry, and yet mesmerized all at the same time. And then, in the middle of the aqua festivities, he saw what appeared to be a figure. His heart was pounding, like it was about to explode through his chest. He rubbed his eyes, which were now bulging out of his head. He was too far away to make out many physical details, but this thing... was a person. The stranger began to look around, as if to get a sense of his or her surroundings. Then they locked eyes. Murphy freaked out and ran his best hundred-yard dash into the bedroom to wake his wife.

"Hey! Wake up!"

"Hmmmph. What? What time is it?"

"You need to see this. Follow me."

Murphy grabbed his wife by the arm and pulled her from the bed, still half asleep. They get to the kitchen and to her surprise... There's nothing there. No bubbles. No person. Just a pool.

"What am I supposed to see?" she asked.

"Wait... Something.... Someone.... Dammit! There was someone out there. I swear!"

"In our pool? Like, swimming?"

"No. I saw bubbles come up again."

"Honey, there's no leak. I had it checked."

"I know. Just... just listen to me. I saw a whole bunch of bubbles, like something weird was going on in the shallow end. And then this thing, this... person. He rose from the center of it."

She just stared at him for a moment before responding. "How do you know it's a he?" she asked coyly. She knew what was going on. He was freaking out, and it was time to dismantle this episode. His brain was playing tricks on him again. Her best guess? He probably had awoken in the middle of a sleepwalking episode.

"I... I'm not sure. I mean... I tried to look closely. It looked like a guy. But as soon as our eyes met, I freaked out and came to get you."

There was clearly nothing there. "I think you're tired. Your eyes are playing tricks on you," she said.

"No, they're not. I swear to God. I saw someone... in the pool."

She wasn't going to argue, but it was time to get him back to bed. They could always discuss it in the morning... if he remembered.

"Come on, baby," she added, as she grabbed his hand to lead him towards the bedroom. They were almost out of the kitchen when he broke away from her grip to take one last glance out of the window, and he saw... nothing.

"I'm not crazy."

"I didn't say you were. Sleep-deprived, maybe. But not crazy. I think you need a day off. You know, to rest."

"Maybe," he concluded, as they made their way to the other end of the house.

Chapter Twelve

"Well, look who's in early today," commented Joe.

Murphy had trouble sleeping, for obvious reasons. That being said, he also had a ton of follow-up work to do after the recent trip, so an early day at the office would help get it all done at a reasonable hour.

"Just getting a jump on things. Not enough time, so much to do."

"Amen, brother. What are you working on?"

"Just getting started on the expense accounts. I want to make sure I don't miss the payment cycle."

"Excellent. Pop by my office when you're done. Let's talk about next steps for the Tulsa trip."

Murphy gave him a thumbs-up. He would say or do anything to get him out of his office, as the expense account comment was a lie. He wasn't logging his expenses. He was online, looking up exhaustion and fatigue, and if it could lead to hallucinations. That really was the only explanation for the previous night. He was seeing things, and he needed confirmation that his lack of sleep could be one of the reasons. Surely there had to be some data to support it. He knew what he saw. But seeing that his wife was not as alarmed as he was... Well... maybe she was right. After all, sleepwalking issues had plagued him in the past.

When he went to see Joe, the door was closed and he was on the phone. So, Murphy made a small request of Amy.

"I need a favor."

"Sure, hon. What's up?"

"Mr. Sterling's birthday is coming up in a month."

"And…"

"I have absolutely no idea what to get him. Do you have any ideas?"

"Not at this moment. But give me a couple of days to think about it. I'm sure I can come up with something."

"Thanks. I want to get him something special, you know, something personal, but I'm drawing a blank."

"It's good you asked me a month in advance. At least we have some time. Unlike Joe over there. He would ask me in the morning when he needs it that afternoon. He may look super organized, but in some regards, he flies by the seat of his pants."

Joe was all about efficient use of his time. Rather than get up and open his door, he threw a pencil at the window to get their attention. He motioned for Murphy to come in.

"So… let's talk Tulsa," Joe began.

"Shoot."

"How did you find this one? Referral? Cold call?"

"Cold call."

"I have to be honest… This one's a bit different than the others."

"Why is that?"

"Because it's a brand-new account."

"Everything we bring on board is a brand-new account."

"No, what I mean is, there's nothing to rollover. No account balances. We make no fee, except for the one to set it up. There's no money to manage."

"Not yet."

"It'll take years for this plant to bear fruit."

"They have to start somewhere. I think it's great that they want to help their employees save for retirement."

"As do I. This is just more of a long-term play. There won't be a lot of commission. I just want to make sure you understand that."

"I understand. I do. It's just, when you cold call, you never know what you're working with. Had they already had an employee investment plan we may not have even had a chance to meet with them."

"True."

"Every company and every investor are different. We sell to their needs. If we do a good job, I can tap into them down the road for some referrals."

"Now that sounds like a successful sales manager. If we close it, and I fully expect us to, I want your commitment that you'll sign every single employee up when you fly out for the install."

"You have my word."

"Great. We're slated for our presentation next Thursday. One day. We fly in, we fly out. No hotel, no dinner out..."

"No gay bars?" Murphy asked jovially.

"Especially no gay bars. Wise ass."

"I'm ready, Joe. We're gonna kill it."

"I know we will. Nice work cultivating this one."

"Thanks."

Chapter Thirteen

"That was amazing!"

Murphy was out of breath after a marathon lovemaking session. "I think we definitely made a baby that time."

"You say that every time we're in bed."

"I know. But this time was different. I did that thing with my legs at the end."

"Oh yeah," she giggled. "That was new."

"Just trying to change things up, you know, to give my swimmers some extra momentum."

"Well, it couldn't hurt."

"If it hurts…"

Mollie joined in and finished his sentence. "…then you're doing it wrong. Ha ha. Could you pass me my drink, please?"

"Too much sex dehydrates you?"

"Apparently. So, not to change the subject…"

"But you're going to."

"Yeah. I'm just curious. You've been on the new job a few weeks now. How's it working out?"

"It's great. I really feel like this is my dream job. I think this gig is really going to put us on a great path."

"Aww, I'm so glad to hear you say that. And working with Joe?"

"We get along great. He's definitely got a different

style than me in terms of client interaction, but it's good for me to experience things from different perspectives. I can see why he's so successful."

"So, no problems being under his wing for the time being?"

"No. Not at all. He's been a great mentor. Although, I have to be honest... We did have an awkward moment when we accidentally found ourselves in a gay bar a few nights ago."

"No! What happened?"

"I had to pretend to be his date so he didn't get hit on."

"Oh. My. God. That is too funny."

"He didn't think so. If you see him again, please don't mention it. I promised him I'd keep that memory under wraps."

"Got it. Well, I'm so happy for you. I know you've wanted this promotion for the longest time."

"Yeah. I have. Life is good, baby. Life is good. You almost ready for bed?"

"My endorphins are raging from rolling around the sheets with you, but I can give it a shot."

After one last drink and a trip to the restroom, Murphy and his bride began their nightly ritual. In the race to fall asleep first, he always came in second place, as Mollie typically passed out almost instantly. It was a gift he was always jealous of. And like previous nights, as soon as she got into a deeper REM cycle, she began to snore, which prevented him from achieving his.

"I've got to buy some earplugs," he thought to himself, as he got up to head into the living room. He parked himself in front of the computer and started playing some random tunes in his media player. His current favorite – a newer hard rock band called Revolution Saints. They had a sound reminiscent of the eighties, one of the greatest decades for music. He logged into his company's VPN and started to fill out his expense report from the day's trip. Though the music wasn't loud, it was enough to mask any sounds coming from the deck just beyond the adjacent sliding glass door. He continued to look at the blinds every few seconds, which were closed for the evening.

"Nope," he said to himself. "I'm not going to look. Whatever I saw wasn't real."

But his curiosity continued to gnaw at him. Or maybe it was his OCD. He leaned over and separated the blinds, only to see a serene scene. A quiet pool deck, a virgin firepit, and still water sitting in the pool.

"Jesus, what the hell am I doing?" He let go of the blinds. "I'm going to drive myself crazy."

He spent the next hour completing his expense account, which would save time in the morning. He glanced at the clock, and noticed it was just past 2am. Maybe Mollie finally stopped snoring. Time to get a few hours of sleep. He got up and walked through the kitchen, but stopped dead in his tracks as soon as his body was positioned next to the bay window overlooking the pool. What he saw in his peripheral view made his heart jump, but he maintained his calm so as not to awaken his wife, who, quite frankly, already thought he was insane. He turned his head and confirmed the sight. Something was glowing in the shallow end. Within the glow was an object, shaped like a person... the same one he had seen the other night.

"A ghost? Is that possible?" he questioned himself. He never really believed in ghosts, but so much of the population does. Maybe they're right? Maybe they do exist. This was an existential event, for sure. Though he couldn't make any logical sense of it, he kept his fear and doubt in check.

The apparition began looking around as if to assess his or her surroundings. Murphy didn't budge, his glare glued to his uninvited guest. And then... their eyes met. They began a staring match, with both trying to assess what the hell was going on.

"Am I dreaming? I must be dreaming. Maybe I'm asleep," he tried to tell himself. But a pinch on the arm convinced him otherwise.

Never one to avoid a confrontation, Murphy initiated the next step, one that would be unparalleled to anything he had done before. He held up his index finger, pointed to himself, then pointed outside. It was his nonverbal way of saying "Hang on, I'm coming out."

He was freaking out, but he knew he couldn't wake his wife. Not without real evidence that something was amiss. He opened the blinds, then quietly unlocked the glass door. He exited the home slowly, at a pace about one-tenth his normal speed, until he came to a stop at the shallow end of the pool. The two of them stood motionless. The spirit seemed as confused and nervous as he was.

"Who are you?" asked Murphy.

The spirit offered no answer.

"What are you doing here?"

It responded nonverbally with shrugged shoulders.

"Where did you come from?"

Again, he answered with a gesture, signifying "I have no earthly idea."

"Why are you in my pool?"

The spirit lifted his hands and watched as the water

rolled out of his palms, as if he was experiencing water for the first time.

"Can you talk?"

"What time is it?" the spirit replied.

The new deck was still a work-in-progress, and as of yet there was no clock outside. Murphy turned to the kitchen window and glanced at the microwave within. "It's 2:20 in the morning."

The stranger nodded his head and continued to look around.

"Are you a ghost?"

"I don't know." Clearly, he was confused.

The apparition lifted himself out of the water and sat at the pool's edge, absorbing every inch of his surroundings as if he was a traveler visiting a new city. His glow disappeared as he exited the pool.

"Do you have a cigarette?" he asked.

"No, sorry. I don't smoke."

Murphy took a few steps back and slowly sat down at the patio table on the lanai. He wasn't sure what was going on, but was, to some degree, paralyzed and couldn't leave. Not without finding out more about his uninvited guest. Unfortunately, it was not to be, as this sighting was about to come to an end.

The spirit lifted his body from the pool's ledge and immersed himself back in the water. "I have to go."

"Go where?"

"Back."

"Back where? You just got here."

As he walked closer to the center of the pool, a few bubbles started to rise to the surface. It looked at Murphy and held up its right hand to wave goodbye.

"Wait! Where are you going?"

He began to submerge within the bubbles and then… he was gone. The water in the pool began to calm until it was smooth as glass.

"There is no way Mollie is going to believe this!"

Chapter Fourteen

"Aww, baby, you look tired. How late did you stay up last night?" Mollie saw the bags under Murphy's eyes and knew he didn't get a full night's sleep. Murphy, of course, was up all night, at first having a conversation with some random apparition, and afterwards, trying to figure out how to tell his wife.

"It was a long night."

"Did you sleep?"

"A little."

"Waiting for bubbles again?" she asked, sarcastically.

He decided to be upfront and very matter-of-fact about the whole ordeal. She was, after all, his partner in life, someone he could – and should – share everything with. "Oh, I saw bubbles. And then some."

"What does that mean?"

"We had a visitor."

Mollie played along. "Aww, your pool pal paid you another visit? That's nice."

"Don't patronize me! I know what I saw."

"And what did you see?"

"Some guy."

"Some guy? What did this 'guy' look like?"

"Stocky frame, dark hair. He seemed a tad older than me. He asked me for a cigarette."

"You don't smoke."

"No shit, Sherlock. I'm just telling you what he said."

"What else did he say?"

"Not much, he was really just looking around, like he was trying to determine his surroundings. Clearly it was his first time here. It was a short visit, then he said he had to go."

"Go where?"

"I don't know. Back to where he came from, I guess. He walked back into the middle of the pool. It started bubbling again, and then he disappeared."

Mollie showed little concern. She tried to play this off as another sleepwalking episode, though this was a little different. He normally has no recollection of any events or conversations, but in this case, he was spouting a number of specific details. He seemed so convinced and she didn't want to call him crazy, so she just offered a simple comment. "Maybe I'll stay up with you tonight, you know, in case he comes back."

That was enough to assuage her husband. "You know what? That's a good idea. Yeah. This whole thing freaked me out. I'd love to have you next to me. I need you to see the same thing that I see."

For Mollie, it was the perfect plan. When they're both together, and awake, and he sees that nobody comes to visit, he would finally see the situation just as she did. "It's a date. You, me, and your new friend. Can I make you some breakfast?" she asked, as she quickly wanted to change the subject to reality.

"I've got to get ready for work. I have no time to sit and eat a full breakfast. Is there any chance you can whip together something for me? Maybe a breakfast wrap while I shower? You know, scrambled eggs, bacon, cheddar? I can eat it in the car on my way."

"I'd love to," she replied, and kissed him on the lips.

Chapter Fifteen

The plan for the evening was to watch the pool area together. But when Murphy saw Mollie sleeping so peacefully, he chose not to wake her. He inched out of bed shortly after 2am and ventured quietly out onto the pool deck. Though he couldn't really explain any of this, he wanted to know more, and the only way was to have him stay longer. In his mind, he was convinced this 'visitor' was a ghost. And if it truly was, then it was a friendly ghost, unlike all of the horror movies he saw. Sure enough, just after 2am, bubbles began to rise from the pool's surface. Murphy was already outside, waiting for his guest. This was their third interaction, and they were no longer scared of each other. The apparition came out of the pool entirely and sat with him at the patio table. For the first two minutes, no words were spoken. Murphy just stared at his guest, who was still looking around, trying to get a grip on where he was. He then reached into his pocket, pulled out a pack of cigarettes and slid them over to his new friend. The spirit took one out, lit it, and took a big drag.

"Thanks."

"Who are you?"

"I'm Pablo," he replied, as he exhaled a big puff of smoke.

"You're Pablo?"

He nodded.

"What are you doing here, Pablo?"

He shrugged his shoulders in reply.

"Where did you come from?"

"I don't know. I just walked through a door."

"A door? Brother, there ain't no door in my pool... Unless my house was built on some old graveyard and you're a spirit who's lost."

"That's the second time you referred to me as a ghost. Is that how you see me?"

"Well, I know you're not real."

"I'm here, aren't I?"

"Are you? Maybe I'm just dreaming, and you're some image I dreamed up."

Pablo touched Murphy with his lit cigarette and burned him on his wrist.

"Ow! What the fuck?"

"That felt real, didn't it? Still think you're dreaming?"

"Maybe not. So, tell me... what's on the other side?"

"The other side of what?"

"The door. You said you walked through a door and showed up here."

"It's hard to explain."

"Try me."

"It's beautiful. It's a place where you're free of pain, free of discomfort, free from the burdens of life. You're just surrounded by unconditional love."

"It's got to be crowded," responded Murphy. "There have to be a ton of people out there."

"Souls," corrected Pablo. "Yes, there are millions."

"You all must be bumping into each other, everywhere you turn."

"You would think so, but the universe is quite large. Infinite, some might argue."

"Do you have any friends out there?"

"There are spirits I have known from my previous life who have passed on."

"With all that spirit traffic out there, you probably never get a chance to see them."

"On the contrary... I can see whoever I want, whenever I want."

"But you just said there are millions of souls."

"As I mentioned before, everything out there is hard to explain. It's only when you're here does it all begin to make sense."

"Do you think my parents are out there?"

"Have they passed on?"

"Yes."

"Then I'm sure of it."

"How come they don't swing by for a visit?"

"Maybe they do. Spirits are not normally detectable with the human eye."

"And yet I can see you, right now."

"I believe that has to do with my purpose."

"Which is...?"

"I'm not quite sure yet. This door to your world was just presented to me recently. I'm not yet able to put it all together."

"Well, if you see them, tell them I miss them."

"I will find them. And I will share your sentiments with them."

Chapter Sixteen

Murphy was the first to awaken the next morning, and began by making a pot of coffee. Mollie joined him about a half hour later, and was immediately bombarded with the previous night's episode.

"We have a ghost in our pool."

"A ghost?"

"Yes."

"In our pool?"

"It appears so."

Mollie nodded her head and kissed him on the lips. She figured this was not unlike some of the previous strange conversations she has had with her man, so she played along. "Excellent. I've always wanted a pet."

"I'm serious!"

"So am I. Did this ghost have a name?"

"Pablo."

"His name is Pablo?"

"Yes. We talked for a couple of hours last night."

Mollie glanced outside. "Out there?"

"Yeah."

"Why is there an ash tray with cigarette butts out there?"

"Pablo smokes."

"Pablo smokes?"

"Yeah."

"So, we have a ghost..."

"Yes."

"His name is Pablo."

"Yes."

"And he smokes."

"Yep."

"Pablo the smoking ghost. Well, that's one for the books."

"You don't seem freaked out."

"Not really. But I am a little concerned about that bruise on your arm. How did that happen?"

"Oh, he burned me with his cigarette. He was trying to convince me he was real."

"Pablo did?"

"Yes."

"Pablo burned you with his cigarette?"

Murphy detected a bit of pessimism. "You still don't believe me, do you?"

Mollie winced her eyes and bobbed her head, which translated to a message of doubt.

"You're coming out with me tonight."

"You said that yesterday, but you never woke me."

"I know. I'm sorry. But you were in such a deep sleep, I felt guilty waking you. I remember the doctor saying that the hormones that trigger ovulation can be impacted by the body's sleep and wake patterns."

"I'm not going to see what you see if you don't wake me up."

"You're right. You're absolutely right. We'll set the alarm tonight to make sure you're up. Just after 2am. I'll introduce you to him."

"2am? Baby, you're going to be tired tomorrow."

"Yeah, I know. But that's when he shows up."

"It's a date. You, me and Pablo."

Once again, his wife was convinced this was all in his head. Maybe tonight she'll be able to convince him, as well.

Chapter Seventeen

Mollie did her part. She stayed up with him every night that week. Five nights had passed with no signs of anything unusual in the pool. No visitor, no bubbles, no activity at all. Mollie was convinced, as she was all along, that there was nothing real to see... except the disappointment on her husband's face.

"Are you ready for bed?" she asked, as the time quickly passed and morning was approaching. "Maybe you can get a few hours of rest before you have to wake up for work."

"I guess so."

"Can we put these sightings to rest now?"

"I don't have a choice, do I?"

"You tell me. There's nothing to see here tonight. And there was nothing last night, and the night before that, and the night before that."

"You think I'm making it up, don't you?"

"You personally? No. I think it's your subconscious."

"It doesn't feel like sleepwalking. You always tell me what I talk about, but none of it ever sounds familiar. I never, ever have any recollection. But..."

"But this time you do. I know, babe. I get it. It's different than the norm. But it's not outside of the realm of possibilities. I can't see any other explanation. Can

58

you?"

Murphy pursed his lips and pondered the question, but in his head, he knew there was only one answer she would accept. And without any proof, if it even existed, he had no choice but to agree.

"C'mon. Let's go inside," he concluded, as he grabbed her hand to head in for a very short night's sleep.

Chapter Eighteen

The next night.

"You're fucking with me!"

Murphy snuck out of bed at 2:30am for a drink, and found his evasive friend on the patio, smoking a cigarette.

"What do you mean?" asked Pablo.

"Mollie waited up every night this week to see you."

"So?"

"So? She thinks I'm seeing things in my sleep. She thinks you're not real."

"Maybe I'm not. Maybe she's right. Maybe I am a figment of your imagination."

"Seriously... let me go get her."

"If you do, I'll be gone when you get back."

"Why are you being such a dick?"

Pablo laughed. "I'm not doing it on purpose. It's the universe."

"I don't buy that! If it's the universe, it makes more sense for you to visit her, not me. She's the one who's into all that astrology nonsense."

"I hate to tell you this, amigo, but it's not nonsense. I used to feel the same way, but the things I've seen... I can assure you, the universe works in ways you can't even imagine."

"Well, this whole thing would be a lot easier on me if you met Mollie. She thinks this is all a dream."

"I don't control the mechanics of when I show up."

"I know. You said there's a light, a door, blah blah blah. Tell me, why do you come here, to this same place, every time?"

"I don't know. I'm sure there's a reason, but I'm not privy to it. Not yet, anyway. Maybe I was assigned to you."

"What does that mean?"

"You know... like the tooth fairy. Everyone gets someone different."

"Everybody doesn't get a different tooth fairy."

"There's so much you need to learn."

"Okay, let's say there's a shred of truth to what you're saying."

"About the tooth fairy?"

"No. Forget the freaking tooth fairy. About you. Why do you think you're assigned to me? Am I in trouble? Are we playing out a modern-day chapter from a Charles Dickens novel? You're here to help me navigate the pitfalls of life and alter my course?"

"I don't know. Maybe it's the opposite."

"You're a very confusing ghost."

"What I mean is, maybe it's you who were selected to help me, and the universe arranged for us to be together."

"Help you? In what way? Are *you* in trouble?"

"I'm pretty sure I'm stuck."

"Stuck where?"

"In limbo. Right here."

"Stuck here? In my backyard?"

"Yeah."

"It's not so bad, if you think about it. I'm sure there are worse places to be than hanging by a pool in Florida."

"You're not getting it. I can't pass over."

"To what?"

"The other side."

"What's on the other side?"

"Eternal peace. Everyone who dies crosses over at some point. I see all these people moving on, and they seem so happy. But I can't."

"Are you talking about heaven?"

"Maybe. I really don't know."

"It's pretty peaceful here, my friend. Stay as long as you want. You can be my guest... my ghost guest. That is, of course, assuming Mollie doesn't have me institutionalized. You really need to meet her."

"I'll try, but as I said before, my movements through the different dimensions are pretty much out of my control. So, do you think you can help?"

"Help what?"

"Me. Pass over."

"Are you serious? How in God's name do you think I can help?"

"There's someone I need to help."

"So just swoop in and help them."

"I just told you... I'm stuck here. This is the only place I can visit. And I can't leave the perimeter."

"What do you mean, you can't leave the perimeter?"

"I tried. It's like there's an invisible line... a wall of sorts, and I can't get past it."

"You're in ghost jail, my friend."

"For lack of a better term, you're right."

"So how do you know that's why you're here?"

"Have you ever seen a line-up of taxi cabs at the airport outside of baggage claim? You know, the first person who needs a ride gets the first ride. Then they all move up. The next person gets the next one, etc."

"Yeah."

"That's kind of like us. For those who can't pass over, we're put into a... hmmm... what's the best way to describe it? A virtual queue."

"A virtual queue?"

"Exactly. And we have to help the next person who needs help. There's never a shortage of people who need help in this world."

"And now it's your turn?"

"It appears that way."

"And you want my help? I honestly don't know any way I can help."

"I'd like to make you my ambassador."

"You can do that?"

"Yes. I need the assistance of someone who doesn't have the same geographic restriction as me."

"My plate's pretty full right now, new job and all. It's pretty stressful. Plus, all of our free time, at least when she's ovulating, is spent trying to start a family."

"So, you can't help me because you're too busy having sex? That should at least be a stress relief."

"You would think so. I mean, yeah, it's fun and all, but it's a different type of pressure."

"What's your favorite position?"

"That's none of your business, spook. You know, you're a pretty nosy ghost."

"Come on! Help me."

"Even if I were willing... how do you propose I do that? You said there was someone in need."

"Yes."

"Okay... Who?"

"I don't know."

"I rest my case. This is futile."

"It's not..."

"Then answer my question: Who? It's not me, is it?

"No, it's not you."

"You're sure?"

"Yes. They were pretty clear about that."

"Okay, well that narrows it down to everyone on the earth, minus one. What does this person look like?"

"I don't know."

"Is there anything you can tell me to help solve this riddle?"

"The spirits can guide us."

"Great. Call 'em up. I'll go get my phone," answered Murphy.

"That's not how it works."

"I know. But I thought it was worth a shot."

"I can tap into their knowledge and guidance, but not in a way that will make sense to you."

"I'm all ears. I can't wait to see how you communicate with this other world."

"They won't tell us. But they can show us."

"This is getting better by the minute. Okay, show me."

"Well, not here."

"Where then?"

"In there," Pablo replied, as he pointed to the pool.

"In there?"

Pablo nodded.

"In the pool? At 4am? Are you out of your freaking mind?"

"I know it sounds crazy, but if we go in together and stand in a very specific position, the water acts as a conduit to the other world and I can share information directly with you."

He stared at Pablo, who had just extinguished his cigarette. "You're serious?"

"I'm certain it'll get me one step closer to peace."

Murphy sat there and considered his request. "I'll make you a deal. I'll go in, if you agree to meet Mollie one night. She thinks I'm nuts, unless I can prove to her that you really exist."

"I can't say when, but I'll try."

"Not good enough. I want your word."

"Okay. If we're successful and I can pass over, I promise I will visit Mollie at some point in time before I go."

"That'll work," answered Murphy, as he pulled off his shirt and walked towards the shallow end. "Let's do this."

Pablo was first to enter the pool. He climbed down the stairs and took a few steps until he was a few feet from the entry and situated precisely in the middle of the shallow end. "So, are you coming in?"

Murphy stood at the water's edge. "I can't believe I'm doing this," he said to himself. He then mimicked his ghost friend's path and joined him in the center.

"Okay. Hold up your hands with both palms facing me, and cross your arms."

"Cross my arms?"

"Yeah, so that your right hand is on the left side of your body, and your left hand is on the right side of your body."

Murphy did as he was told and held up his hands. Pablo then followed the exact same steps and crossed his arms so their palms were facing each other.

"This is ridiculous," said Murphy.

"Shush. This will work, but it has to be exactly as I say. Now we touch palms. Your right palm connects with my left palm, and your left palm connects with my right palm."

"Do we lock fingers?"

"No... we just make sure our palms connect to each other."

"Okay. Done. What's next?"

"One of your feet now has to touch mine."

"Are you sure there's no hidden camera? This is, by far, the dumbest..."

"Do it," Pablo interrupted.

"Fine." Murphy moved his left foot forward, so that inside of his foot was touching the inside of Pablo's left foot.

"Now what?"

"We close our eyes and ask for help."

"This is stupid."

"Murphy... you have to trust me. They will reach out to us. I know they will."

They were now standing in a strange position, like two puzzle pieces that were just snapped together. It was an odd stance, but what Murphy couldn't yet grasp, they just built the equivalent of an antenna that somehow, miraculously, connected with some other dimension. They closed their eyes and Pablo began speaking.

"*O, forti universum, ut vocarent te: ostende nobis, ut nos videre non possunt.*"

Thirty seconds had passed, when out of nowhere, a few bubbles began to ascend from the base of the pool around them.

"Holy shit, something's happening," said Murphy.

"Shh. Yes, it is. Remain silent and let it happen."

This was, without a doubt, the craziest thing Murphy had ever done. But it worked. With bubbles brewing around them, an image became apparent to both of them.

"Do you see the same thing I do?"

"I see a building, not a person," replied Pablo.

"Okay, me too. I thought you said you had to help a person?"

"I do. Maybe the person is inside the building."

"That would narrow it down a little, wouldn't it? Will they show this person to us?"

"It doesn't appear so. They're just passing along this one, static image."

"So, where's this building?"

"I thought you might know."

"Nope. It doesn't look familiar to me. Are they able to scan the area? Maybe there's a marker or sign or something else that might provide a hint."

And just then, the image went dark. They had hoped to glean information who they should help, and were beamed a photo of a strange, old building instead.

"I think that's all we're going to get," said Pablo, as the bubbles receded.

"I'm sorry," said Murphy. "I just don't know where that is."

"It's okay. If it was meant to be, the answer will uncover itself."

"If you say so. By the way… what did you say before? Was that Latin?"

"Yeah. '*O, forti universum, ut vocarent te: ostende nobis, ut nos videre non possunt.*' It means 'Oh, mighty universe, we summon thee, to show us what we cannot see.'"

"You speak Latin?"

"I speak all languages. We all do. Spirits come from all over the globe. It's a barrier that's removed when you die. Communication is never an issue."

"So, when you die, you get retrofitted with a universal language chip?"

"Something like that."

"Well, they certainly heard you. That was a pretty neat trick."

Pablo's left shoulder jerked backwards.

"Are you okay?"

"It's time for me to go."

"But you'll be back, right?"

"I can't go anywhere else, until you find the building and help me help someone."

The split-second Pablo disappeared, Murphy heard his wife scream. "Oh my God, Murphy! What the hell are you doing in the pool?! Wake up, baby! Wake up!"

Murphy was awake, but paused for a moment to play out a few scenarios in his head. "Don't say it," he said to himself. "Don't say the ghost made you do it. Just don't. No good can come of that, and she definitely won't believe you." But he could never lie to his best friend. At some point in time, she had to believe him. Didn't she?

Mollie put a towel on him and quietly walked him to bed, the same way she concluded all of his sleepwalking episodes.

Chapter Nineteen

"Can we talk about last night?"

Murphy sat quietly on a stool next to the breakfast nook. He knew this conversation was imminent. "Sure."

"I'm worried."

"Baby, there's nothing to worry about."

"Nothing to worry about? You were in the pool at, like, four in the morning."

"There was a reason."

"Because from my perspective, you went swimming while you were asleep."

"I wasn't asleep."

"Really? So, how would you like to explain this?"

Murphy looked right into his partner's eyes. It was as if he chose to answer that question telepathically.

"No," she replied angrily.

"Hon…"

"Don't you dare say it!"

"I swear to God. This is the absolute truth. I was talking with Pablo…"

"Are you fucking serious?! You're going to tell me that your imaginary friend told you to get in the pool?"

"Well, for starters he's not imaginary. And secondly, there was a reason we went in. Would you like to hear it?"

"Oh my God. My husband is insane. He's swimming with ghosts! I can't believe we're having this conversation."

"Babe…"

"No, don't 'babe' me. This is serious, Murphy!"

"I'm treating this as serious as you are."

"Are you? Because from where I'm standing, you're asking me to believe that something in your head…"

"It's not in my head, Mollie. Pablo is real."

"He's not fucking real! It was a dream! Murphy! Wake up! I love you, but listen to yourself. We do not have a ghost in our pool!"

The argument was futile. He knew it. There was no sense in continuing it. She would never see his point of view. At least not today. "I have to go to work," he concluded abruptly, as he got up and left the kitchen.

Chapter Twenty

"Amy," began Joe, "do me a favor… Sterling is asking for a progress report."

"And…?"

"I'd like you to send an email to each of the new sales managers. Ask each of them to send a summary of what we've done together since they've been promoted. How many accounts have they worked on, how much money have they brought in for us to manage and then ask them for their commitment of what they'll deliver in the next fiscal quarter. I'll put all the responses together for one update."

"Sure. Due when?"

"Tomorrow. End of day."

"I'm on it."

"Thanks."

As anticipated, one day later, he had three emails in his In Box from his sales managers. Two of them laid out the exact details he had requested. Murphy, being the unique spirit that he was, chose to answer the request differently, and attached a sound file instead of a written document. The email contained one sentence: *Attached is a summary of our time together.*

Joe double-clicked the MP4 and listened intently.

"Amy," he shouted. "Get Murphy in here. Now!"

Amy poked her head around the corner of Joe's door. "And if he's busy?"

"Now!" he demanded.

"Yes sir."

Within minutes, Murphy was sitting in Joe's office with a goofy grin.

"Oh, you're hysterical," Joe began.

"I'm just fooling around," replied Murphy. "Here," he added, as he handed Joe a real, written summary of their time together. "I thought you'd get a laugh out of how I spliced them all together."

"You're a hoot."

"I knew we had a unique relationship, especially after that encounter at that Nashville bar."

"Oooh, what happened in Nashville?" Amy asked, as she entered the office to drop some mail on Joe's desk.

"Sorry, Amy. What happens on the road, stays on the road," Joe replied.

"Come on, play it for her," Murphy requested. "You're a good sport."

"You're lucky I am," he replied.

Joe double-clicked the icon and the three of them were treated to a summary of Joe's road rage, spliced together from a dozen different trips.

"I enjoy driving to gigs. It's very peaceful. Move! Left lane is for passing, you donut head! Come on, old man! Pick up the pace! Fuck! Damn it! Go through the yellow, go through the yellow! Ugh! You suck! Asshole! Nice turn signal, Mr. Fancy Car! A turtle! I'm stuck behind a turtle! Damn it! Fuck me! Fuck you! Are you kidding me?!? Moron... you could've made the light. Seriously?!?! Why would you get in front of me and then slow down? Idiot!

Is there a snail convention in town? Move! The light's yellow... Go! Go! Go! Crap! Dumbass! I enjoy driving to gigs. It's very peaceful."

The three of them enjoyed a good laugh, at Joe's expense.

"Okay," said Joe. "Fun time is over. Everyone back to work."

Amy departed for her desk, leaving Murphy in the office.

"Keep that sense of humor, Murph. You never know what curveballs life will throw at you."

"You got it boss. Everything you need is in the letter. Any questions, let me know."

Murphy then left and walked through Amy's reception area, taking note of an image on her computer.

"What's that?"

Murphy was getting into the grind of another work day and approached Amy for some assistance with some copying.

"What's what?"

"That. On your computer."

"It's a website."

"Wow, Einstein can't hold a candle to you. You're brilliant."

"You asked me to help find something to give to Mr. Sterling for his birthday. He's into exotic coffees, and I found this really cool place. It's about a half-hour away. They seem to have some of the most diverse beans in the state."

"Actually, that's a really good idea," Murphy replied, as he looked closer at some of the pictures on the site. "It looks like an old place, must have been around for years" he added, as he pointed to one of the pictures. "Click that one."

Amy clicked and was brought to zoomed in photo of the signage. It was washed out, like it had been there for decades and weathered many a Florida hurricane. And it probably had. He scanned some of the other pictures and saw that it was housed in a standalone, historic-looking building.

"Wait... That building. Where is that?"

"It's about a half-hour away, why?"

"That building looks familiar. Why does that building look familiar?" he asked himself.

"It's in Ybor City. Have you ever been there before?"

"No. But I've seen it... in my..." and he stopped himself when it finally clicked.

"Dreams," said Amy.

"What?"

"You said you've seen it in your... I thought you were going to say dreams."

He felt no need to add anyone else to the list of people who thought he was crazy, and answered appropriately. "Travels. I was going to say in my travels, smarty-pants."

"They do online orders. Do you want me to order you a gift card for Mr. Sterling?"

"No... I'm actually going to be out that way later in the week. Maybe I'll stop in."

Maybe? Wild horses couldn't keep him away. The universe was steering him to this hole-in-the-wall coffee bar, tucked away on a side street in historic Ybor City. Of course, he was going to stop in.

Chapter Twenty-One

"Why do you always come out at 2:00am and leave a couple of hours later?" asked Murphy.

"Actually, it's a little shy of two hours. I come out at 2:14am. And I depart at 3:57am," replied Pablo.

"That's pretty specific. Does it have any significance?"

"I have no idea. Wherever I am, that's when some type of portal opens. The only way I can explain it is that it's a light…"

"It's always a light. 'Head into the light, Carol Anne.'"

"Are you mocking me?"

"No," he chuckled. "Go on."

"Well, I go to the light, and somehow I mysteriously end up here."

"In my pool."

"Yes. And then… it's hard to explain… as much as I'd like to stay and talk to you all night, there's some type of force that pulls me back an hour and forty-three minutes later."

"An hour and forty-three minutes?"

"Every time. It's always an hour and forty-three minutes."

"It's got to mean something."

"Your guess is as good as mine."

"Well, we have just over an hour and a half left.

75

Anything in particular you'd like to do? I mean, I know you're stuck here, but we can still make the best of it."

Pablo smiled. "You know what I miss?" he asked, as he began reminiscing from his previous existence.

"No, what."

"A cold glass of milk. And ice cream."

"I have both. Would you like some?"

"Wow, that would be great. If it's not too much trouble, of course."

"No trouble at all."

Murphy retreated into the house, making sure to tip toe and not make a sound. A few minutes later, he returned holding a tray with the requested items.

Pablo put a spoonful of ice cream in his mouth and closed his eyes, allowing himself to savor the moment.

"What flavor is this?"

"Vanilla bean."

"I know it's vanilla. It tastes different than I'm used to."

"Maybe because it's fat-free?"

"Fat-free ice cream? Yeah, that's the culprit."

"You don't like it?"

"It's fine. It just lacks... I don't know... full flavor."

"Then you're not going to like the milk, either."

"Fat-free milk?"

"We call it skim."

"Please... it's colored water."

"Too much fat isn't good for you."

"Do you really think I'm concerned about my health? I'm already dead."

"Do they have grocery stores where you came from?"

"I haven't seen any."

"Exactly. This is what Mollie buys, and it's all we have in the house. It's either this or nothing. Take your pick."

"This is fine. I'll make it work. It's just... well, in my previous incarnation, I owned a restaurant. I was the chef, so flavor was always important to me."

"That's pretty cool. I always wanted to learn how to cook."

"I loved cooking. That was my passion. My restaurant was always busy. Had a lot of repeat customers, too."

"Mollie does most of the cooking. I only do it every now and then."

"Did you enjoy it?"

"I did. It started out a little bumpy. I had a garlic episode one time, while Mollie and I were dating. She always likes to tell that story when friends come over."

"A garlic episode?"

"I confused the term 'bulb' with 'clove.' It was an honest mistake."

"Oh my God!"

"I cooked Baked Ziti. I was trying to impress her. The recipe called for four cloves of garlic."

"But you used four bulbs?"

"Yeah."

"So, that was like, forty to fifty cloves of garlic."

"She likes garlic, and commented it was very garlicky."

"Did you tell her?"

"No! I thought I knocked it out of the park. But then she commented a few days later that no matter how many times she showered, she still smelled like garlic. Apparently, it came out of her pores for days. She asked me to describe my recipe to her, and that's when I discovered a bulb and a clove were two different things."

"How did she react?"

"It took a little while, but she eventually agreed to go out with me again. But only if I took her *out* to dinner."

"So, you don't cook?"

"Very little. I grill a bunch. You know, steaks and burgers."

"My favorite dishes were blending seafood and Mexican."

"That doesn't sound appealing."

"Au contraire! People went crazy for my grouper tacos and grilled shrimp burritos. You just have to give them a try. Bring out a notebook one night. I'd love to share some recipes with you."

"I'm not sure she'll give me carte blanche in the kitchen."

"Ask her for one more culinary chance. I promise, you will impress her."

"Thanks. I will. Hey… can I ask you a personal question?"

"Sure."

"How did you die?"

Pablo offered a sullen look. He pulled out a cigarette and held it in his hand. "You sure you want to know?"

"Everyone dies at some point. It's one of the few certainties in life."

"Yeah. That, and taxes."

"I'm just curious. You don't have to tell me if you don't want to."

"The same way over thirty-thousand people die every year. In a car accident."

"Really? Drunk driver?"

"No. It was just a freak accident. I swerved to avoid hitting something in the road and hit a tree instead. I don't remember anything after that, so I'm guessing I died pretty instantly."

"That sucks. I'm sorry to hear that."

"You have to figure, with over two hundred and fifty million cars on the road each year, accidents are bound to happen. It was just my time."

"How long ago was that?"

Pablo smiled and finally lit his cigarette. "You know what? I really don't know."

"No clocks or calendars in the afterlife?"

"I guess it's just weird. Time has no meaning here. I've been here a while. I just don't know how long."

"If you had the chance to come back and share what you've learned, you know, for the short period of time you were alive... what would you say?"

"Life advice?"

"Yeah."

Pablo thought for a moment. "Try new things. Do the things that scare you. Don't be afraid of uncomfortable situations. They build character. And fail. Fail spectacularly. That's the biggest motivator in life."

Murphy and Pablo continued talking for however long the universe let them be together. Their time outside was beginning to take on new meaning. Their conversations became very personal. They were no longer random souls who met in the middle of the night. They were becoming... friends.

Mollie awakened and noticed Murphy was not in bed with her. She looked at the clock. 3:56am. She got up to look for him, though she knew she wouldn't have to look hard as there weren't many places he could go. At

79

3:57am, Pablo said goodbye and departed for the evening. Within seconds, Mollie turned the corner and wandered into the kitchen. And then she saw it. Her husband, sitting alone at the patio table by the pool, with three cigarette butts in the ash tray and a half drank glass of milk. "Murphy, Murphy, Murphy..." she said to herself. "What the hell is going on with you?" She chose to turn around and head back to bed, rather than confront her husband, as those conversations were never productive.

Chapter Twenty-Two

A few nights later.

"I'll take two." Pablo laid two cards face down and pushed them towards the deck. He and Murphy were playing poker. No stakes. Just a casual game among friends.

Murphy slid two cards off the top of the pile. "Here are your two, dealer takes one. What do you have?"

"Two pair. Aces and Nines. You?"

"You win. I was pulling for the flush but missed the last spade on the draw. Your turn to deal," he said, as he pulled all of the cards together into single pile and passed them across the table.

"I missed you yesterday," said Pablo as he began shuffling the deck.

"I had to fly out of town for work."

"How was the trip?"

"The trip itself was great. We closed the deal. And it has some great potential, so the firm was happy. But the flight out was really bumpy. We hit a lot of turbulence. That always freaks me out."

"You know what causes that, right?"

"Turbulence? Yeah... air pockets."

"Nope. It's us."

"Us? What do you mean, us?"

"Us. The spirits. That's how we get around. The speed at which we can travel increases with the altitude. There are millions of ghosts out there, zipping around. Your ride was bumpy because you hit a spirit pocket. A spocket."

"A spocket?"

"I know what you're thinking... it's not a real word. But that's what we call it. You know... when you combine two words into one. Your plane went through a densely populated pocket of spirits."

Murphy sat there and attempted to process that statement. "It is not! You are so full of shit! That's not what causes turbulence!"

Pablo started to laugh. "I know. But you should have seen your face, trying to look up 'spocket' in your mental dictionary. That was priceless."

"You're a ghosthole," he replied. "That's what we call a ghost who's also an ass..."

"Yeah, yeah, yeah," Pablo interrupted, as he dealt the next hand. "But you closed the deal, right?"

"We did. You want to hear a funny story?"

"Sure."

"It's kind of appropriate, since we're playing cards right now."

"You helped a poker champion invest his winnings?"

"No, but close. We met with the owner of a radio station in Tulsa. WDRB. This kid, he looked to be in his mid-twenties, he recently won the station in a card game."

"Wow. Big stakes."

"Yeah. He said they played a low-limit game quite regularly, but this one escalated quickly. It was a crazy story. When we met, he said he wanted to do something special for the staff to not only help them save money, but to assist with employee retention. So, we pitched a retirement plan that he's going to help fund with company profits."

"And you, of course, made something off the deal, right?"

"Well, yeah. I get a commission. But in this case, it's relatively small since they're just starting out. And there's not a lot of profit since he just took over and doesn't really know what he's doing. But his heart is in the right place. The firm gets a fee for setting up the account, and as the balances grow, we continue to earn income on managing the funds."

"Good for you. Congratulations on closing the deal."

"Thanks. Oh, by the way... I finally figured out where that building was."

"Really? Did you go there?"

"Tomorrow. I'll let you know how it goes."

Chapter Twenty-Three

It was a cute little place, housed in a historic building that had to be at least a hundred years old. But the inside was modern. And cozy. The perimeter was lined with couches and ottomans. There was a small bar area, though no alcohol was served, only coffee drinks. The back wall was lined with two dozen transparent tube-shaped containers filled with beans from all over the world. Want a cup? They grind enough for one cup at a time, if you choose. Art from local artists adorned the walls, each with its own price tag, as it was all for sale. Murphy continued to look around, soaking in the environment.

"Can I help you?" asked a young girl behind the counter. Murphy acknowledged her with a smile.

"Sure. Yeah... do you sell gift cards?"

"We do."

"Great. I need one for a hundred dollars."

"Wow, that'll buy a lot of coffee."

"It's for my boss. He's a coffee nut."

"Then it's the perfect gift. Can I get you anything else?"

Murphy stared at the drink board off to the side. "Yeah, how about a large, regular coffee, with skim milk and sugar-free vanilla syrup?"

The young girl placed a metal scoop under one of the tubes and with a simple pull of a lever, released enough beans to grind for a large, non-fat coffee.

"Here you are. And here's your gift card."

"Thank you," he replied, as he handed over his credit card. Upon completing the transaction, he turned to grab a seat on one of the vacant couches, when, out of nowhere, he was punched in the face by a man standing behind him.

"You son-of-a-bitch," shouted the stranger. The force of the punch knocked Murphy on his ass, causing his hot beverage to spill all over his freshly pressed shirt. "I'm going to take great joy in suing your ass off," the stranger continued.

It took a few moments for Murphy to refocus his eyes and he quickly noticed his assailant looked familiar. "I know you."

"You're goddamn right you know me."

"Mr. Wainwright. You attended one of my financial seminars."

"I did more than that! I gave you a check to invest. My life savings, over eight-hundred and fifty thousand dollars."

"I'm confused."

"Well let me clarify the situation for you, you prick! You didn't do what you said you were going to do."

"We invested your funds."

"Sure. You did. You put the whole fucking check into some type of bullshit space exploration fund. My life savings is now invested in companies that plan to land on comets and drill for minerals."

"A space fund?"

"Does that conversation sound familiar? Because it doesn't to me. You put me into something that comes

85

with way more risk that I was willing to take. What the fuck happened to stocks and bonds? Where's the diversification you promised?"

"Mr. Wainwright, I'm so sorry. There's obviously some type of mistake. Let me go back to the office and get this fixed for you."

"You better. Or I'll not only sue you, I'll file a complaint with the SEC and you'll never work in finance again!"

Wainwright departed, leaving Murphy bewildered. He had no idea how that could have happened. He always ensured any and all investments met the needs of the investor. All details were mutually agreed upon prior to moving forward. It had to be Joe. He wasn't sure why, or how, but there was no other explanation.

He went back to the register to grab a couple of napkins to dry his shirt. "Any chance I can get a refill?" he asked, as he handed his empty cup to the girl. "I didn't get a chance to drink the first one."

"Sure," she answered, without asking any other details. "Are you okay?"

"Yeah. I'm fine. He just caught me by surprise."

"You want some ice for your eye? It looks like it's starting to bruise a little."

"That's not a bad idea. Thanks."

The girl turned to grab a small bag from a cabinet and walked over to the ice machine. Murphy was still trying to figure out what the heck went wrong, when he heard a scream.

"Somebody help!!! He's choking!!"

Murphy turned and saw an elderly man with his hands around his throat. His wife was hitting him on the back, trying to dislodge whatever was stuck. Murphy looked around and saw nobody was moving, so he jumped into action, dropping his coffee in the process. He ran over, lifted the elderly gentleman from his seat, and immediately began to do the Heimlich maneuver.

"Please... please help him," the old woman whimpered.

"Come on, friend. Spit it out," said Murphy, as he began applying sudden and firm pressure to his ribcage. The moment seemed to go on forever, but in reality, it lasted only about twenty seconds, with a large chunk of donut being expelled at the end.

The old man was frightened and out of breath, but he knew the worst was behind him. He collapsed in his seat and looked up at Murphy. "Thank you."

"You okay?"

"Yeah. I am now."

"Thank you so much," added his spouse. "We've been together over fifty years. I'm not ready to lose him yet."

"Today's not his day," he replied, with a smile. "Can I get either of you anything? Glass of water?"

"No... we're fine. I'm so thankful you were here today. You saved his life."

"I did, didn't I?" he thought to himself. "I can't believe that spook was right." Suddenly his mood had changed. Sure, he still had an unhappy investor. But he would deal with that tomorrow. He was now flying high. He walked back over the counter to grab some more napkins to wipe up the mocha puddle from when he dropped his second cup of coffee. And then went for a third.

The young girl smiled. "You sure picked an interesting night for your first visit. One more cup?"

"Sure. Let's see if I can actually drink this one."

"Third time's a charm," she said with a big smile. "That was a beautiful thing you did. You saved his life."

"Sometimes it's just a matter of being in the right place, at the right time."

"Here," she started. "Here's a coupon for a free coffee drink the next time you come in. As a thank you."

"Running a special, are you? Save a life, drink for free?"

"The world would be a better place if that were the case, don't you think?"

"I do," he replied. "Thank you. This is a nice gesture. And thanks for the refill."

"Enjoy your night. And thanks for the good deed. Karma will remember this moment, and will return the favor when you least expect it."

"I hope you're right," he replied, as he put two dollars in the tip jar. "I can use all the good karma I can get."

Murphy walked over to one of the vacant lounge chairs to sip and enjoy his third cup of coffee, which, ironically, was really his first. He was interrupted every few moments by other patrons, offering praise for his quick action. He saved a life. Pablo's going to be so excited.

Chapter Twenty-Four

"What the heck happened to you?"

Murphy came home from work as he always does, but today he was sporting a fresh bruise under his left eye.

"Long story," he began. "I went to a café in Ybor to buy Sterling a birthday present. I ran into one of my investors who wasn't happy where we put his money."

"That's assault. You should have had him arrested."

"Well, there's a little more to his story, but let's just say he had every right to be angry. I'll take care of everything at work tomorrow morning. Oh, but the craziest thing happened."

"Besides being assaulted?"

"Yeah. I saved this guy's life."

"What?! What happened?"

"I heard a woman start to panic, she yelled that her husband couldn't breathe. Apparently, he was choking on a donut. I ran over there and started doing the Heimlich."

"Oh, my God! Murphy, that's amazing. I'm so proud of you. Wow, that's a lot of excitement in one day."

"You're telling me."

"I think you need a beach day, you know, a day to just chill."

"That sounds therapeutic."

"You and me on the Causeway, this weekend. It would be so relaxing."

"That would be fun. Count me in."

The two got ready for bed, and like most nights, Mollie passed out almost instantly. Murphy snuck out of bed at 2am, poured some milk, grabbed an ash tray, and prepared for a night with his friend.

"You've seen better days," said Pablo, referring to Murphy's face. "What happened?"

"It was a crazy day. I went to that café, you know, the building we saw. I ran into one of my investors."

"Did he lose money on one of your investments?"

"No, but... had his money gone where it was supposed to, everything would have been fine. But my boss crossed an ethical line and changed funds without telling me."

"Crossed an ethical line? That sounds serious."

"I'll move the money tomorrow."

"Sounds like you need to have some words with your boss."

"I'm sure he had his reasons."

"That's not the point. You need to confront him."

"He's my boss. And Sterling loves him. I'm afraid if I make waves, it'll be me who's shown the door."

"Doesn't matter. It's like that scene from 'Scarface.' All you have is your balls and your word. He may be your superior, but you've got to stand up for yourself. You gotta stake your turf, Murph."

"You're probably right. Oh, by the way, in other news... I saved someone's life tonight."

"Really?"

"Yeah. That whole scene in the pool paid off. I did it. You can move on now."

"Wow, Murphy.... Thank you so much... I can't tell you how much that means to me."

"Just one friend helping another."

"Cheers," replied Pablo, as he held up his milk.

Chapter Twenty-Five

"We need to talk. Right now!" exclaimed Murphy, as he barged into Joe's office.

"Okay, shoot."

"Wainwright."

"I see your Wainwright and raise you a Masterson."

"No. Mr. Wainwright. Donald Wainwright."

"Name sounds a little familiar."

"I ran a financial seminar, he cut us a check for eight-hundred and fifty thousand dollars to invest. Is it starting to sound a little more familiar?"

"I know who he is."

"I ran into him yesterday. He's pissed."

"Is that where you got your shiner from? That looks like it hurt."

"He cold-cocked me in a coffee café."

"Ha! Say that three times, fast."

"Joe, I'm serious. What the fuck? Why did you change his investment? Without consulting me or him? He's threatening to file a complaint with the SEC."

"I wouldn't worry about that. We get a lot of threats."

"We need to move his money."

"We can't."

"Why not?"

"Because it's in a specialty fund. It has to stay there for a minimum of six months. It's contractual."

"Jesus, are you serious?"

"You're not looking at the big picture here."

"I'm not? We're in a business based on trust and referrals. And we screwed him."

"We didn't screw him."

"How would you explain it, then?"

"His money's safe. Well, yes, it's in a fund that may carry some unusual risk. But the chances of him losing it all are slim to none. In fact, last time I checked, it was up almost two percent. Compared to the S&P, I think his investment is doing quite well."

"That's not the point."

"I know. The point, which you are failing to recognize, is that particular fund comes with an annualized expense fee of 0.75%. It's a little high, but not outside the norm for a specialty fund. For this particular quarter, they're running a broker promo. One-half of that expense fee for the first year of investment is converted into commission. Do the math. $850K times 0.75% is what?"

"Just over six-thousand dollars."

"Six-thousand, three-hundred and seventy-five, to be exact. Fifty percent of that is ours. You and I just earned three grand on one sale. That's in addition to our normal commission."

"Joe, it's not about the money."

"Yeah, rookie. It is. It's all about the money. That's why we're in this business."

"I'm moving the money."

"I told you, you can't. Not for six months."

"Fine. As soon as six months hits, I'm moving it."

"Stop being so dramatic. Once six months hits, you can do anything you want. I'll have moved on to bigger fish. And you will have, too."

Though Joe was wealthy and a top performer, Murphy was now learning why. And he was pissed. What he did may not have been illegal, but it certainly was unethical. Murphy was starting to learn that not every footstep Joe took should be followed. He thought back to his conversation with Pablo and pulled the trigger. He took one step closer and made his declaration. "Don't touch my clients' money. Got it? What you did was a shitty move, and it's got my name and more importantly, my reputation all over it."

Joe took a step closer, as well. "Sorry to tell you this rookie, but we're a team. Until Sterling decides you're ready to go out on your own, all of *your* gigs are *our* gigs, like it or not."

"Not."

And just then, Mr. Sterling, the CEO of Sterling Investments, walked by and saw the two of them talking.

"Looks like there's a lot of testosterone in this room. Gentlemen... is everything okay?" he asked, after noticing that they were speaking unusually close to each other.

"Yes sir," answered Joe. "We were just discussing differences in opinion regarding investment strategy."

"Always a productive conversation," replied Sterling. "Murphy, it would be wise to listen to everything Joe has to say. He's one of the most successful sales people this firm has ever employed. You're lucky to have him as your coach and mentor."

"Yes sir. Lucky, indeed," he replied, without breaking eye contact with Joe.

"I'm sure you'll come to the right decision with your investment. Remember, the customers' needs always come first. Carry on, gentlemen," concluded Sterling, as he departed the office.

Joe sat back at his desk and continued the conversation with his underling. "You'll need to get over this. And soon. We have a lot more business to do together. Don't like working with me? There's the door," he claimed, as he pointed to the entrance of his office.

Murphy still would not break eye contact.

"Look, here's my suggestion. If you want to smooth things over, send Wainwright a note and tell him there was a misunderstanding with his risk tolerance and you'll pull the money out as soon as you're able to. But also make sure to point out how much money he's made so far. Almost seventeen-thousand dollars. Better-than-expected gains normally erase disappointment. You'd be surprised. Once people see how they're taking advantage of the stock market, and doing better than average, many ultimately decide to keep the money where it is."

"He was really upset."

"Risk and reward, Murph. That's what we balance. Risk and reward. You made him money. And, at the same time, you made some for yourself. That's the game we play. Is that all you wanted to talk about?"

Murphy knew the conversation was over. He wasn't happy, as this was not a decision he would have made. But what was done, was done, and he had to live with it. "Yeah, that's it."

"Put some ice on that shiner, brother. It'll heal quicker. And close the door on your way out. Thanks."

Chapter Twenty-Six

"Did we bring my baseball hat?"

"Oh, yeah, I popped it into the beach bag," replied Mollie. "Here," she said, as she pulled it out and handed it to him.

"I gotta protect my head. Rumor has it I have a bald spot."

"It's a little more than a rumor."

"Well, to be honest, I've never seen it."

"That's because it's on the back of your head."

"If I can't see it, maybe it doesn't exist."

"What about those pictures we took?"

"Which ones?"

"From Charleston. I took it from behind... while you were watching them make candy. That showed a bald spot."

"Pictures can be doctored."

"Is that what I did? Took a bunch of vacation photos and threw a filter on them to thin out your hair?"

"Hey, I don't know what you do after I go to bed at night. It's possible."

"Keep singing that song, baby. But put on your hat while you're doing it. You know... just in case."

The two enjoyed a relaxing Saturday on the Dunedin Causeway, a two-and-a-half-mile road connecting part of Pinellas County to the beautiful beaches of Honeymoon

Island. With water views of the St. Joseph Sound and plenty of free parking along the way, the Causeway was a popular destination for fishing, walking, bike riding and sunbathing. Though they had a nice pool and enjoyed it frequently, they still attempted to hit the beach once or twice a month. There was something therapeutic about listening to the sounds of the tiny waves splashing against the sand. Murphy sat in his chair with a notebook, mapping out an action plan for the coming week. His bride? She enjoyed playing on her tablet, reading articles and exchanging text messages with friends near and far. He was scribbling away when his concentration was suddenly interrupted.

"Uh oh," said Mollie.

"What?" he replied.

Her response was delayed as she continued to scroll through her present topic. He chose not to inquire any further. If it was important, she would tell him. But chances are, it wasn't. It was usually a text from a friend regarding a topic that he had no interest in. A single girlfriend had a bad first date. An overweight gal pal discovered a new diet. Or... his favorite... something caught her eye in her horoscope.

"Can I read something to you?" she asked.

"Sure. Go for it."

"So, Mercury's in retrograde..."

"Horoscope. I knew it. This ought to be good," he said to himself. He wasn't one to believe in those things, but she did, so he always listened quasi-intently when she felt there was something worth sharing. "Is that a good thing or a bad thing?"

"You can't paint it with such a broad stroke," she replied. "It affects all signs differently."

"All twelve of them?" he laughed. "So, you can paint one-twelfth of the population with a broad stroke, just not everyone. Got it."

"Are you going to let me finish? Or are you going to continue with your nonbeliever rant?"

"I'm sorry," he added with a smile. "Go ahead."

"I'm reading my monthly summary. It says a family member is entering into a challenging time, and it requires the patience and understanding of family and friends to help them through it."

"And...?"

"Maybe it's you."

"Me? Oh, come on!"

"Maybe it has to do with your recent sleepwalking. You haven't walked in years. The last time was when? Four years ago?"

Murphy paused briefly to reminisce in his head. "Yeah, when dad died. And we had to go through all that legal crap to settle the estate."

"Right. It's when you're stressed. Maybe this new job is more stressful than you expected."

"No," he laughed. "It's exactly as stressful as I expected."

"Seriously."

"Hon, the job's not that stressful. I can totally do it. The quarterly boards come out in a week, and I fully expect to be in the top ten percent."

"Just because you're successful at it doesn't mean it's not stressful," she added.

"True."

"I think my horoscope is dead-on. So, what can I do?"

"What do you mean?"

"To help. You know, alleviate some of the stress."

"I can think of a few things. But first, that bikini's gotta come off."

"Ha ha. You know I'm not ovulating, right?"

"So? We have to limit our intimacy to when you're ovulating? I want to start a family as bad as you, but maybe that mindset is unconsciously adding to some of the stress."

"So... Random sex is the answer?"

"I'm a guy. To many of life's quandaries, yes, sex is the answer."

"You're crazy," she said, as she leaned in for a kiss. "But I still love you."

The Causeway was getting crowded, as it always does. While they were talking, a family parked next to them and began setting up their beach chairs.

"Check out that little guy," exclaimed Mollie. "He's so cute."

"Aww, he looks like he's two years old."

"He's making a beeline for the water."

"Jimmy," called out his mother, "come here Jimmy. Don't get too close to the water."

"Jimmy's at the beach," Murphy uttered to his wife. "He ain't gonna listen."

"Wow, look at him go."

The random mother tried one last time. "Jimmy... Look what GG has for you."

"Oh, look. He stopped" exclaimed Mollie.

"I hope GG has something good," he replied.

"He's actually thinking about it. Look at him trying to process it all with his little brain. That's adorable. Head to the water...?"

"Ha! Or see what's behind door number two."

"Jimmy! I have a cookie."

"He turned around! That's great!"
"The cookie wins, every time."
Mollie smiled. "I can't wait to have kids."
"Me too, babe. Me too."

Chapter Twenty-Seven

Mollie went to bed early, as a day in the sun always exhausted her. She enjoyed it, for sure, but she was pooped. Murphy stayed up, partly because he wasn't tired and partly because, well... he saved somebody's life. He wanted to be sure Pablo did not show up, which meant he had successfully achieved his goal. But that wasn't the case.

"Did you forget something?" asked Murphy.

"No," replied Pablo.

"Because if I'm understanding things correctly, you should be on your way to an afterlife party."

Pablo offered only a saddened face. "That wasn't it."

"What?! What do you mean, that wasn't it? You said you needed to help a random soul."

"I know."

"And you said I could be your ambassador."

"I know. I know. But that wasn't the event they were referring to."

"How do you know?"

"Intuition. Signs. I just... I got a message. It doesn't matter how I got it. I just got it. I have to keep looking."

"This is un-fucking-believable. We saved a life. How much more are they expecting?"

"The random act was great. Right place, right time. You're a hero. Don't minimize it. But in my journey, it's very specific. And that wasn't it."

"That's crap!"

"I know, but... can we drop it, at least for now? Let's change the subject."

"Sure. What would you like to do?"

"We can just chat."

"Okay. About what?"

"What was the last movie you saw?"

"That's what you want to know?"

"Sounds trivial, I know, but I miss that. I miss date night with my wife."

"We stream a lot. And watch DVDs quite often. The last one was last week. We saw 'Good Will Hunting.'"

"I saw that. Great flick."

"I wasn't going to say anything, but since you brought up movies..."

"Go ahead."

"This feels eerily like 'Field of Dreams.'"

"What does?"

"This! This whole situation. Me and you."

"Did strange voices tell you to build the pool?"

"No, of course not."

"Do you have unresolved issues with your dad? Maybe he'll pop up one day and ask you to go for a swim?"

"No... it's just... you're here, inexplicably, you can't leave the premises... I'm just saying... there are similarities."

"I guess... that was a really good flick. Have you ever seen 'Butterfly Effect?'"

"That was a good one, too. The sequels were just okay, but the original had a great storyline."

102

"Do you believe it?"

"What? In time travel? No… not possible."

"No, I mean the overall theme. You know, the tagline. Change one thing, change everything."

"I don't know. I never really thought of it."

"I do. All the time. I mean, look at me. Had I not gotten into that car that night…"

"The world is full of 'what ifs,'" replied Murphy.

"I know. But hear me out. Had I not gotten into that car, on that night, I quite possibly might still be alive today."

"True. But there were no signs, right? There was nothing leading you to believe that would happen."

"No. No premonitions or anything. But the bottom line is still true. Had I changed that one thing on that one night…"

"When it's your time, it's your time. You said it yourself."

"I know. It still sucks."

Murphy put his hand on Pablo's shoulder in an act of comfort. "We'll get you there. I know you're stuck. But we'll get you there. I promise."

Chapter Twenty-Eight

"I didn't expect to see you again," said the young lady behind the register.

"Why's that?"

"Well, the last time you were here, you got beat up and then saved someone's life. I figured you had enough excitement. We saw more action that night than we see all year."

"It was a pretty eventful night, wasn't it? Nah, I'm just on my way home from work and thought I'd pop in for a drink. Everybody here is so friendly, and work was... well... let's just say I can use a few friendly faces."

"What was that about?" she asked, as she poured his cup.

"What?"

"That fight. Why did he attack you?"

"Like you, I'm in the service industry. He wasn't happy with my service. It wasn't a big deal. Just a misunderstanding. I rectified the situation."

"You hang with a pretty rough crowd if that's how you all express your dissatisfaction. You're not going to break my kneecaps or torch my apartment if I forget to put creamer in your cup, are you?"

"No," he smiled. "You're safe."

"So, your customer is happy again?"

104

She didn't need to know all the details, as they barely knew each other. He kept his reply short and sweet. "He is." Murphy paid for his drink and dropped the change in the tip jar sitting on the counter.

"Thanks! I can use all the help I can get. My car's in the shop."

"Uh oh! I hope it's not serious."

"I have to replace something called a serpentine belt, whatever that is."

"Yeah, you need that. But it shouldn't be too expensive. It's common to replace those at least once in a car's lifetime."

"I'm hoping they don't find anything else and I can pick it up after work today."

"My fingers are crossed for you."

"Thanks. Enjoy the coffee."

"Thank you."

Murphy left the counter and scanned the area for a place to sit. It really was a relaxing and casual atmosphere and had a steady flow of customers. He sat in a lounge chair off in the corner which offered a unique vantage point that allowed him to view the entire establishment. He then thought back to his previous night with his poolside poltergeist, and the puzzle they were trying to solve. Somebody needed help, and that person was somehow associated with this cafe. He glanced around and estimated there were around two dozen individuals present. Part of the problem was, many folks didn't stay long. Sure, there were some who brought a laptop or a book and parked themselves for an hour or two. But others came in, made their purchase, and left. It increased the number of candidates and made it impossible to determine every single person's situation, and who might be in some sort of predicament that required guidance or assistance.

A student sat in the corner with a stack of books, presently reading a guide on LSATs. Maybe he needed help getting into law school. An elderly couple was relaxing on a couch in the opposite corner. Maybe they needed assistance with everyday tasks. A middle-aged man was sitting at one of the high tops, reading a newspaper. Maybe he was scanning the classifieds and needed help finding a job. The possibilities were endless, again, making the task in front of him virtually impossible. But he forged on and began to work the room, moving from one spot to another.

His first stop was a couch, situated in front of a television with the sound muted. This put him in proximity to the prospective law student.

"That's a tough exam," he commented, making reference to the LSAT book the young man was reading.

"Have you ever taken it?"

"Me? No. My folks wanted me to go into law, but I chose finance instead."

"Good money in finance?"

"It pays the bills. What's that big book next to you? It's huge."

"Just something I have to become familiar with."

Murphy glanced over and saw the chapter number written at the top. "Does that say Chapter Seven-Hundred and Seventy-Six?"

"Yeah."

"Wow, there's a lot of chapters in there. What's that one about?"

The student passed the book over to him, rather than explain its contents. Murphy held the large tome in his hands and began reading. "Oh, okay, I got it," Murphy replied, as he passed the book back. "So, what type of law interests you?"

"Criminal. I'm probably going to get arrested one day. I'd like to be able to represent myself."

Murphy thought to himself, "that's an odd statement." But he wished him well and moved on to another spot on the other side of the room. He was listening in on a conversation with two young ladies, pretending to admire the original paintings on the wall in front of him.

"Did you call the police?" one girl asked.

"Yeah. But they weren't so optimistic I would get my stuff back. But they did notify the local pawn shops with the serial number of my laptop and camera, so the items would be flagged if someone tried to pawn them."

It didn't take long for Murphy to put two and two together. One of the young ladies was burglarized. What a shame.

"The cop said the same thing to me," commented the other girl.

"You were robbed, too?"

"Yeah. About a month ago."

"That's an odd coincidence," he thought to himself.

There was a steady buzz of conversation in the café, which was interrupted by a comment from the counter area. "No! Are you serious?" He glanced over and saw the young girl who served him, disappointed with whomever she was speaking with on the phone. His best guess? Either the mechanic found something else wrong with her vehicle, or it wasn't going to be ready when she originally thought. Upon hanging up, she began walking the café and clearing some of the tables, until she came to the one next to Murphy.

"That didn't sound good."

"What?"

"The phone call. News on the car?"

"Yeah. They can't get the belt until tomorrow morning."

"I guess that's better than the alternative, you know, if they found other things that needed to be fixed."

"You're a glass-is-half-full kind of guy, aren't you?"

"I try," he replied with a smile.

"You're probably right. Unfortunately, I have no way to get home, so I'm kind of stressed right now."

"I'm getting ready to head out in a little while. I could drop you somewhere on my way, if you'd like."

"I'm not sure my momma would be thrilled, you know, getting into a car with a stranger."

"You're right. It's probably best if someone you know takes you home. I'm sorry. I didn't mean to stick my nose where it doesn't belong."

"Thank you anyway," she replied, as she continued her quest wiping down the tables.

Murphy went back to pondering his puzzle, trying to determine who needed a good deed, which, in turn, would allow his friend to move on. An hour had passed, two coffees consumed, when he decided it was time to go. Unfortunately, he was no further along in his quest. He would have to figure it out another day. He brought his empty cup to the counter and said goodbye to those up front when his server peeked her head around the corner.

"Hey," she said. "You leaving?"

"Yeah. It's time."

"Is the offer for a ride still good?"

"Sure. But it doesn't change the fact that I'm still a stranger."

"Hi, I'm Jordan," she said, as she offered her hand for a shake.

"Murphy," he replied, as he shook her hand.

"See? Strangers, no more."

"You sure you're comfortable with this?"

"Yeah, I'm fine. You saved someone's life. You're a good soul." She turned her attention to her co-workers. "I'm heading out. I'll see you all tomorrow."

"Bye, Jordan," they all chimed back.

It wasn't a gesture of great significance. It wouldn't send Pablo on his way. But Murphy needed all the good karma he could get and felt any good deed can only help.

It was a short drive, as Jordan only lived a few miles from the café. They filled their ten minutes together with random conversation.

"That's a pretty unique tattoo," commented Murphy.

"Which one? I have a couple."

"The one on your right wrist. I noticed it when we shook hands."

"Yeah. I love that one. It was my first ink. It's a Chinese symbol for 'family.' My family means the world to me."

"Same here."

"Thanks for the lift. I really appreciate it. I'm getting together with a bunch of folks in the apartment complex who are taking the same class as me. We're doing a study session at seven. I didn't want to miss it."

"Happy to help. Where do you go to school?"

"USF. I'm a sophomore."

"Good for you. School's important. What's your major?"

"I'm presently undecided," she giggled. "Right now, I'm majoring in coffee, with a minor in crumb cakes."

"That's okay. What's important is that you're going. You'll eventually figure it out."

"Yeah, that's what my mom said, too."

"She must be proud. You seem like a hard worker, balancing out a job and college," he added, as he pulled into her parking lot.

"It's not easy, that's for sure. But I'm getting it all done. Oh, there's my place. 203."

"I'll wait here until you're safely inside. Have a good night. Good luck with your study group tonight."

"Thanks…" she replied, as she pulled out her keys. "And thanks for the lift. You're a lifesaver." She walked over to the building and climbed the stairs to the second floor. Murphy waited to pull away, and it was a good thing he did, as she had trouble opening her door. She leaned over the railing and made a sad face.

"What's up?" he inquired, as he rolled down his window.

"Door's stuck. Happens from time to time. Can you help me? I promise it'll only take two seconds."

Murphy turned off the engine and climbed the stairs. "Have you mentioned this to the apartment manager?"

"Yeah. I filled out a service request. I'm still waiting for them to come down."

Murphy jiggled the key and turned the knob, but also had no success. He started pushing on the outside of the door, thinking maybe there was something causing it to be stuck.

"What about that window?"

"What about it?"

He walked over and tried to open it from the outside.

"Just checking. It's locked."

"Well, of course it's locked. I don't want to give a robber an easy way in."

He began to use his body weight on the door, and eventually it opened.

"That was harder than I thought. You need to call the maintenance guy and get that fixed."

"I will."

"Seriously. Like, immediately. That's not safe. What if you have to get out in a hurry?"

"You sound like my mom."

"And?"

"I'll fill out another maintenance request online tonight. Is that soon enough?" she asked.

"And make a call, too. Cover all your bases."

"Yes sir."

"Have a good night, Jordan."

"Thank you, you too."

.

Chapter Twenty-Nine

Monday morning.

"Good morning, Melissa. Nice weekend?"

Melissa returned to work after a rare weekend off with her spouse.

"Yeah, it was great. Jeff and I were finally able to coordinate a couple of days off together."

"It's hard in this line of work," commented her coworker. "It's definitely not a Monday-through-Friday, Nine-to-Five gig. Where did you wind up going? Last I heard, you were trying to go somewhere special for your anniversary."

"We did. Believe it or not, we stayed kind of local. We were only an hour away in Sarasota."

"I love Sarasota," said Mike, who jumped in on the conversation. "Where did you end up staying?"

"On the beach. Lido Key."

"Very nice. Were you able to spend some time at St. Armand's Circle?"

"All day yesterday. What a fun place to walk around."

"Glad you had a good time."

"Not as good as the criminals in Tampa did. That's a pretty big pile of case files on my desk."

"Mondays are always busy. Crime doesn't take the weekend off."

"I get it. It's just... that looks bigger than normal."

"We like to call that job security. Welcome to Tampa."

"Any priorities that need immediate attention?"

"A couple of them are flagged. Captain thought they might be related to a couple of open cases we have floating around."

"Alrighty, then," she replied. "I'm on it. Oh, and Russell?"

"Yeah?"

"You owe me a slice of pecan pie."

"What?"

"Don't play innocent with me. I know it was you who stole it from my lunch bag."

Russell looked at her with a perplexed look on his face.

"Dude, we work in a crime lab. Your prints were all over my lunch bag!"

"You lifted my prints?" he asked, in astonishment.

"Ha! You are so busted," cried Mike. "Hand it over!"

"Hand what over?" she asked.

"Fine," replied Russell, as he pulled a five-dollar bill from his wallet.

"You bet against me?"

"In my defense, they put me up to it."

"Mm hmm. So, what did we learn from this silly little test, boys?"

"Don't fuck with Mel."

"Bingo. Now, go away. I have work to do."

Melissa began her workday as she often does, by reviewing evidence from recent criminal activities. She parsed out her workload and spent the morning focusing on scanning fingerprints. That task often provided the fastest ROI. If she got a hit, well… it normally meant she was able to get one more criminal off the streets.

She was halfway through her backlog when she came across something strange.

"Huh. That's impossible. That can't be right."

She picked up the phone and dialed the number in the case file.

"Hillsborough Police Department. How may I direct your call?"

"Officer Lumpkin, please."

"One moment, I'll transfer you."

Ring, ring…

"This is Lumpkin."

"Officer Lumpkin, hi. My name is Melissa Banks. I work over in the crime lab. Do you have a free minute to discuss one of your recent cases?"

"Sure. Which one?"

"Case file 01-1762-47B."

There was a moment of silence on the phone as the officer sifted through some papers on his desk.

"Here it is. It's a burglary. What's your question?"

"Is it possible it got mixed up with something else?"

"I was the responding officer. When our tech came out, they found three unique sets of prints and documented all three. Did you not get them all?"

"I did. I just wanted to verify that all three were recorded from the scene in question. Thank you."

"Thank you, Officer Banks. Please call back if you have any other questions on this case."

"I will."

Melissa hung up the phone and had only one thought running through her head. "Well, this ought to be interesting."

Chapter Thirty

A few days later.

Knock, knock!

Mollie answered the door, and to her surprise, she was greeted by her friend, Jeff. This in itself wasn't unusual, as they were friends. But he was dressed in full police garb, ready for work, and he had his partner in tow.

"Hi Jeff," she said. "Happy Wednesday! To what do I owe the pleasure of this visit?"

"Is Murphy home?"

"Yeah. Is… is everything okay?"

"We need to talk to Murphy."

"Okay, sure. He's getting ready for work. Hang on one minute, let me get him."

"Well, this looks ominous," commented Murphy as he entered the room. "What's up, Jeff?"

"Can we talk to you outside for a sec?"

"Yeah, sure."

Mollie was confused, but if it were important, her husband would fill her in later.

"We need you to come down to the station," said Jeff.

"For what?"

"Questions."

"In relation to…"

"We're not at liberty to say just yet. We just need to bring you in and ask you some questions."

"Bring me in? It sounds as if I'm being arrested. Jeff... am I... am I in trouble?"

"I'm sure it's nothing. Come with us, and we'll have you back here in an hour or two."

"Okay," he answered nervously. "Let me make a quick phone call to work and let them know I'm going to be late."

"What do they want?" asked Mollie.

"I have no idea. They won't tell me. They just want me to go with them to the police station."

"You think this has anything to do with the fight you got into at the café?"

"Your guess is as good as mine. I'm sure it's nothing," he added, as he kissed his bride. "I'll be back soon."

"Okay. Good luck."

Murphy got into the back of the cruiser and they departed for the police station.

"Jeff... you mind if I ask you a personal question?"

"Not at all. What's up?"

"Have you ever pulled your gun?"

"Sure. I've had to break leather plenty of times."

"Break leather?"

"It's slang. It's when you draw your gun from your holster. It all depends on the situation, of course. It's not something we do blindly. When our gun comes out, it's because the situation calls for it."

"Of course. That makes sense. Have you ever had to use it?"

"Are you asking me if I've ever shot someone?"

"Well... yeah."

116

"To be honest... no. I have yet to be in a position where I have had to discharge it because someone's life, or even my own, was in danger."

"I have," interrupted Jeff's partner.

"Really?"

"A few years ago. I was answering an armed robbery call, and one of the suspects pointed a gun at me. I had only a split-second to act."

"Wow," replied Murphy.

"Jeff's right," he continued. "It always comes down to the situation. I was in one where my life was in imminent danger. It was him or me. Thankfully I squeezed off a couple of rounds before he did."

"Did you try to disarm him? Or did you shoot to kill?"

"Shoot to kill is not a phrase we use. We are trained to stop the threat and eliminate the danger as quickly and safely as possible. We aim for the largest target, which is the torso. Center mass."

"Which can kill a person."

"Often times. But it gives us the best chance at connecting and ending the threat."

"Interesting. Hopefully, neither of you are threatened by me sitting here in the back seat."

"Chill, Murph. You're safe. Neither of us are planning on shooting you."

"Unless you keep asking questions," his partner replied, sarcastically. Jeff smiled, and Murphy rode out the rest of the trip in silence.

Two hours later, as promised, Jeff brought Murphy back to his residence.

"What was that about?" asked Mollie.

"It's crazy. Apparently, my prints matched a crime scene they were investigating. No big deal. I have to get ready for work," he concluded, as he turned to walk away.

"Whoa, whoa, whoa. Hang on one sec, cowboy. What crime scene? And why are your fingerprints in the police database to begin with?"

"It's part of the licensing requirements for the financial industry. Standard practice. All of our prints are in the database."

"Okay. Now back to the crime scene comment you made."

"There was an apartment that was burglarized."

"Where?"

"Over in Ybor."

"Why would your prints be in an apartment in Ybor?"

"I took one of the workers home. From that coffee café I went to. Her car was in the shop."

"You took a girl home?"

"Yeah. Hon, it's no big deal."

"Is that why you're home late every night?"

"I see where you think this is going, but…"

"How old is she?"

"Mollie…"

"How old?"

"I don't know. Seventeen? Eighteen? Mollie, it's not what you think. This is totally innocent. I would never cheat on you, you know that." He then added a little sarcasm, knowing his wife could take it. "Besides, you and I are having sex, like, seventeen times per week. I may be virile, but a man has his limitations."

"That's not funny."

"Oh, come on. It's a little funny."

"You've been spending an awful lot of time at that café lately."

"It's a really cute place. I'll bring you down there one day. You'd love it in there. Seriously, there's nothing to worry about."

He was careful to not say a ghost in their pool asked him to go on his behalf. He certainly learned his lesson. Some things are better left unsaid.

"Are we good?"

"I guess."

"Thank you. I need to go pack. I have a trip to Atlanta tomorrow."

"With Joe?"

"Nope. He's finally letting me fly solo, at least for this one gig."

"Good. I don't know why he has to shadow you anyway. You're the star player at that place."

"Actually, I'm shadowing him, but you're right. I don't need supervision. I never did. That was all Sterling's idea."

Chapter Thirty-One

Though the gig in Atlanta went great, it also went past the scheduled time, forcing Murphy to rush to the airport to catch his flight.

"You didn't need to run," said the young lady at the gate.

Murphy was breathing heavy from his sprint and squeaked out his reply between gasps. "Why... don't tell me... the flight is delayed."

"No sir."

"Thank God."

"It's cancelled."

"No! Are you serious?"

"Yes sir. A freak snowstorm in the northeast grounded hundreds of flights. Your plane was grounded before it had a chance to leave LaGuardia."

"And this was the last flight to Tampa?"

"Yes sir. I'm sorry. The earliest we can get you out is tomorrow morning. Would you like me to book you a seat on the 6:15am flight?"

"Might as well," he replied, as he looked around at all of the people who were in the same predicament. "What do you think the chances are in finding a hotel room this late at night?"

The airline employee tapped away on her keyboard until the computer spit out a new boarding pass. "You can certainly try, but... there were a lot of flights cancelled."

That effort was, of course, futile. If he was going to get any sleep at all, it was going to be in the airport. It wasn't a common occurrence, but when one travels as much as he did, one is bound to run into that situation every now and then.

"Thank you for the boarding pass. I might as well go stake my turf."

"You're welcome. Have a good evening, sir."

He grabbed his bag, loosened his tie, and walked toward the end of the concourse where the herd of angry, stranded passengers was much thinner. He then pulled out his phone to give his bride an update.

"Hey babe."

"Hey, hon. You at the airport?"

"Yup."

"Late night. But at least you'll be home in a couple of hours and get to sleep in your own bed."

"Nope."

"What do you mean? Oh, don't tell me..."

"Flight was cancelled. Bad weather up north. My plane never made it down here."

"Oh baby, I'm so sorry."

"It's fine. I'll be on the first flight out tomorrow morning."

"Can you get a room?"

"That would be nice, wouldn't it?"

"So, that's a no?"

"I tried. No, I'm just going to hang out here. It'll quiet down in the next hour or two and I'll find myself a nice comfy bench."

"Well, try to get some rest. I love you."

"I love you, too. I'll see you in the morning."

He took one last trip to the bathroom and then sauntered over to a vending machine to buy a bottle of water to quench his middle-of-the-night thirst which seemed to hit just about every night.

The evening's bad luck continued when, during the purchase, his water bottle got stuck between two rungs as it was falling. "Are you serious?" he said, as he pounded on the front of the machine.

"Stuck?" asked a random female passerby.

"Stuck here, stuck there."

"You think if I buy one, it'll fall on top of yours and they'll both come out?"

"If you're a gambling gal, we can certainly try."

"I'm pretty confident," she replied. She inserted her coins, made her selection, and as predicted, both bottles fell to the bottom for retrieval.

"Good call," he said. "Thanks. I'm Murphy."

"You're welcome, Murphy. I'm Monica," she replied with a smile, as she twisted off her cap. "So, are you here for the night?"

"Apparently."

"Me too."

"Were you here on business? Or pleasure?"

"A little of each. A friend threw a party."

"That's nice. What type of celebration was it? Bridal? Birthday?"

"Psychic."

"A psychic party? Really? You believe in that stuff?"

"I hope so. I'm the psychic."

"Get out! That's your business?"

"Yes sir. I sat with each person for a half hour…"

122

"And told them their future?" he asked, with a chuckle.

"Hey, I'm very good at what I do. Plus, these parties are good money."

"Well, if you ever want to invest that money," he said as he handed her a business card, "give me a call."

"That's what you do?"

"Yes ma'am. People entrust me with their money so I can make them more money."

"But you don't believe in psychics?"

"Me? Not really. My wife? Definitely."

"What if I told you something about yourself, something I couldn't possibly know. Would you still be such a pessimist?"

"You're gonna read me?"

"If you're up for it."

"I was curious how I would pass the time tonight. I guess this is as good a plan as ever."

"Okay. Let's sit. Someplace quiet... away from everyone."

He pointed to the end of the concourse. "How about there? Gate Forty-Two."

The two of them walked over and made themselves comfortable in a couple of chairs.

"Take off your wedding ring," she began. "I can normally pull a lot of information that way."

"Sure." He twisted it off and handed it to her. "Go for it. Read me."

She recognized his doubtful attitude, as she had seen it many times before. She clenched the ring tight in her hands and closed her eyes. "Okay... you're married."

"Duh."

"You adore your wife."

"Double duh. I thought you were going to tell me something you couldn't possibly know?"

"Relax. I'm getting there. Okay... you and your wife are happy. You have a wonderful relationship. In fact, you're both happy most of the time. But..."

"But what?"

"You both want something. Something you can't buy."

His ears perked up.

"And that upsets you, because you would give her the world. And this... this one thing is not only out of your reach, but out of your control."

In his mind, Murphy was thinking "did she just pull our troubles getting pregnant out of thin air? A total stranger?"

"But the sex is good. And frequent," she concluded.

"Yes, she did."

"Did I read you?" she asked with a grin.

"Like a book. Okay, if you have this innate ability, can you answer the question?"

"Which question?"

"Will it happen?"

"I thought you said you don't believe in psychics."

"Let's say I'm turning the corner."

She closed her eyes again and squeezed the ring even tighter. She remained silent for about thirty seconds. "I can't tell."

"It was a no, wasn't it? You just don't want to give bad news."

"No, that's not it. The message I'm getting is strange. It's like it's being blocked and certain things have to happen before the message will present itself."

"That makes no sense. What things have to happen?"

"I don't know. The answer is there. I just can't get to it."

The two of them made themselves comfortable down by Gate Forty-Two. They had plenty of time to kill, and they weren't going anywhere until morning.

"How do you connect to these visions?"

Monica had her eyes closed and was resting on the floor, using a rolled-up sweatshirt as a pillow.

"What?"

"How do you connect to these visions?"

"You mean, how can I see things?"

"Yeah."

"They just come to me. But that's not the question you really want to ask, is it?"

"You're pretty good," he replied.

"Go ahead. Ask."

"Do you ever see things in your sleep?"

"Do you?" she asked, turning the tables on him.

"No, no... I was just curious. This whole psychic thing is new to me."

"A lot of it has to do with intuition. We're all intuitive, some are just more so than others. And still others, like myself, develop these intuitive powers into full psychic ability."

"It's a gift," he said.

"A gift for the masses, for everyone is blessed with intuition."

"Interesting," he said, as he sank back into his chair, deep in thought.

Hours later.

"Looks like everyone is lining up."

125

"Yeah," she replied. "Did you sleep okay?"

"Barely."

"Me too. I'm going to go grab some coffee and jump in my queue. Would you like some?"

"No, I'm good. But thanks for asking."

"It was a pleasure sleeping with you... so to speak," she said, in a humorous tone.

"Same here." Murphy reached out for a handshake, a confirmation of a new friendship. While gripping his hand, Monica's face turned to one of concern. "Are you okay?"

She closed her eyes and held his hand with both of hers.

"Monica?"

"Hold on, one moment."

She stood, silently, for about twenty seconds. "I'm sorry. Something just jumped out as I held your hand."

"Must be an occupational hazard, always seeing things when you meet people."

"You have no idea."

"Is this something you want to share?"

"I'm sensing there's a rift at work. Some type of confrontation between you and a coworker."

"Wow, you are good. Yeah, there was... but I addressed it. It's all worked out."

"I don't think so."

"What do you mean?"

"There's a storm coming. I see it getting worse. A lot worse. I'm sorry, Murphy. I normally don't like to share bad news, but this kind of jumped out at me."

"Is it possible you're wrong? I mean, yeah, it was an issue. But it's been fine since then."

"Just keep your eyes open. Something is on the horizon. I don't know what it is, but it's big."

"Thank you. I appreciate the concern."

She replied with a smile. "Safe flight, Murphy."

Chapter Thirty-Two

Mollie had a busy day in front of her, so she wanted to get her household chores done early. Her first task was to tackle the laundry. She carried the basket of dirty clothes into the laundry room and ran the water. She threw most of the contents into the washing machine in a clump, but went piece-by-piece when it came to her husband's garments. He always left something in his pockets, so she took the extra step to ensure they were empty before dropping them in. Typically, she found loose change, sometimes a tissue or a napkin. Today she pulled out a business card. *Monica Stephens – Psychic.*

"What the heck is he doing with a card from a psychic?" she thought to herself. "He doesn't believe in that stuff." She attempted to reconcile those particular pants to the day of the week when they were worn, and came to the conclusion, based on all of the wrinkles, that those were the pants he slept in at the airport. She was sure they met randomly... but given the challenges she has had with her spouse and his escalation in sleepwalking episodes, she thought this might be a sign. A sign to reach out and maybe get some type of reading, maybe some guidance. Even though her husband didn't believe in psychic readings, she did. So, she called.

"Hello?"

"Hi. Is this Ms. Stephens?"

"It is. Who do I have the pleasure of speaking with?"

"You don't know me, but my name is Mollie. I think you met my husband last week at the airport."

"Your husband is Murphy."

"You remember him?"

"He's hard to forget."

"It's funny… he's not really a believer in psychics and readings and such."

"He told me. But I think if you were to ask him now, he might think otherwise."

"Really? Did he hire you to do a reading?"

"Not really. Let's just say we had a productive conversation, and he's less of a pessimist."

"Oh, okay. That's interesting."

"You're worried about him, aren't you?"

"You can tell that through the phone?"

"Sweetheart, when the messages come through this strong, it's hard not to see them. What seems to be bothering you, hon?"

"Yeah… I am worried. He's… well… he hasn't been himself lately."

"He's a good man, Mollie. But you're right to be worried. He's seems to be in the middle of an unusual cycle of lunar activity."

"Can you tell me that in English?"

"Something's going on in his life. I'm not exactly sure what, but it's big."

"Is it work related?"

"Here's where it gets interesting. Yes, there is something going on at work, but from what I'm able to gather, something is happening at home, too. I just don't know if one is the cause of the other, or if they're mutually exclusive from each other. Does that help?"

"Is this period of lunar activity something we'll be able to get through, you know, in one piece?"

"I mentioned to your husband that there are answers out there, but I can't see them. It's not that they don't exist. They're there. But they're being blocked."

"I don't understand."

"It's like you're sitting in traffic waiting to cross the street. You don't know if it's safe to cross because there's a car in front of you, blocking your view. Once the car's gone, you can see everything clearly. Right now, there's something blocking my view. I can't see across that street."

"I see."

"What I can tell you is that when this all comes to a close, both issues will conclude at approximately the same time."

"You're referring to the work issue and the home issue?"

"Yes. That's what I see."

"Thank you. That helps. I think. Can I ask you a random question?"

"Sure."

"When you get your visions… do you… I mean… do they ever come to you in your sleep?"

"Wow!"

"What?"

"You two are completely in sync."

"Why do you say that?"

"Because he asked me the exact same question."

"Did he? That's really interesting."

"I can tell you two belong together."

"Aww, thank you. Yeah, he's the love of my life."

"Mollie, who is Robbie?"

"Who?"

"Robbie. The name keeps popping up."

"I don't know. It doesn't sound familiar. At least, not to me."

"Mollie..."

"Yes?"

"I don't know you or your husband, but this event, all the signs are pointing to something big, something unlike anything you've encountered before. I don't mean to scare you or anything, but he needs you. Now more than ever. It's family and friends that will get you all through this."

"Thank you. I really appreciate your time."

"Please call, if you have any questions. Seriously, no charge. I'm concerned and if I can offer even a shred of guidance, I'd like to help."

"I appreciate the support, Ms. Stephens. Have a nice day."

"Thank you, Mollie. You, too."

To say Mollie was a tad freaked out was an understatement. But she knew what was going on, as she was a key player in this chapter of their life together. And this phone call was confirmation that she saw things exactly as they were. Murphy's in over his head at work, and it's impacting his sleep patterns, which were causing him to sleepwalk and hallucinate. There had to be a solution.

Chapter Thirty-Three

Back at the café.

"Hey stranger," said Jordan, as she greeted Murphy.

"Hi there."

"So, I guess I owe you an apology."

"For what?"

"I heard the police brought you in for questioning when my place was broken into."

"Oh, that. Yeah, that was weird."

"They contacted me and asked if I knew you. I mentioned how you helped me get in one night and your fingerprints were all over the door and window."

"My wife completely flipped out. The police showed up at my door, wouldn't say why, and brought me down for questioning. When I tried giving her an abbreviated version, she was like 'Why are your fingerprints at a crime scene in Ybor?'"

"She wasn't happy, huh?"

"She's fine now. She just didn't know the whole story. You know, none of this would have happened, if your door worked properly."

"I know, I know. They fixed it."

"Good. Anyway, I told the police the same thing you did. I gave you a ride home, your door was jammed, blah blah blah. No big deal."

"Well, I am sorry for the inconvenience. Can I offer you a free cup of Joe for your trouble?"

"I'd like that. Thank you. So, was anything stolen?"

"Yeah, it's so frustrating. They took some jewelry, my phone, and my mom's watch. I think I'm most upset about the watch."

"Well, sure, because it's personal."

"It was really cool. The face was a Kennedy half dollar, and the coin was minted the year I was born. She gave it to me on my sixteenth birthday."

"That's quite unique. I'll bet if you searched around online, you could probably find another one."

"Yeah, but this was special. Because it was hers."

"I get it. A nice keepsake."

"Yeah. And the phone... well, you know, that's just a gigantic inconvenience. I use it for everything... calendar appointments, maps, reminders..."

"And phone calls, right?" he added with a chuckle.

"Yeah, that too. The problem is they're so freaking expensive. I need, like, one or two more paychecks before I can buy a new one."

"Could you get by with something used?"

"I'd hate to buy a used one. I know they're cheaper, but I'd ultimately be buying someone else's problems."

"What if it were in good condition? Would you be able to use it temporarily, until you had the chance to get a new one?"

"I guess."

"I have a couple of older models at home. We never got rid of them when we upgraded. We figured they'd be good as a backup, in case we ever needed one. I can bring one in, if you want. You can use it until you have the money to buy a new one."

"That's a really nice gesture. Thank you."

"You'd still have to get it activated, you know, with your own phone number. But then you'd be able to keep in touch with your world. And your mom."

"My mom is my world."

"Well there you go. I'll bring it by tomorrow."

"You really are a kind soul."

"Just trying to pay it forward."

Chapter Thirty-Four

Mollie was laying on the couch, head parked in a pillow at one end, feet massaged by her husband at the other.

"I have a confession to make," she commented, breaking the silence in the room.

"What's up?"

"I was doing laundry earlier and I found a business card for a psychic in your pocket."

"Oh, yeah. Monica. Nice woman. She was stuck at the airport overnight with me last week. We chatted for quite a bit."

"I called her."

"You did? Why?"

"I don't know. I guess, well, curiosity got the best of me. You know me, I'm always up for a reading, if the person is truly insightful. And you and I, to be honest, with your sleepwalking and all… I don't know, I guess I just wanted some spiritual guidance."

It was an interesting admission, but not one that bothered him. She's seen psychics before. And if she was able to hear something that might help put her mind at ease, well, it would be a win for all involved.

"And…?"

"She mentioned something about a conflict at work. Maybe that's what's causing you to walk."

"She mentioned the same to me. Actually, I was quite surprised she pulled that out of thin air. There was something going on at work. Between me and Joe. It was a little heated for a while, but I took care of it."

"She said it was big."

"I think she exaggerated a bit. But you don't have to worry. I confronted him, stood my ground, and it was resolved."

"So, it's no longer an issue?"

"No... it's no longer an issue."

"Okay..." That was enough to appease her for at least fifteen seconds. Until she chimed in one last time. "Who's Robbie?"

"Robbie?"

"Yeah. She mentioned that name kept popping up, but didn't know why."

"Interesting."

"Why is that interesting. Do you know a Robbie?"

"Sort of. I mean, we have a Robbie at work. But he wasn't involved in what was going on between Joe and me. In all honesty, we actually don't really interact that much."

"What was the issue?"

"I don't want to bore you with details from work. It wasn't a big deal, really. I took care of it. One and done."

"Okay, so I shouldn't worry?"

"Nope. Work is great. Smooth sailing from here on out."

She heard his words and wanted to find comfort in them, but she was still leaning on the pessimistic side. There were far too many mornings where she woke up to playing cards, drinks and extinguished cigarettes on the lanai. He was still sleepwalking, and the episodes were occurring with more frequency. She accepted his answer, but in her heart, was convinced it may only be a partial truth.

Murphy ended the evening in his study, preparing for some upcoming presentations.

"Do you have a lot more to do?" Mollie asked.

"Not much. Are you going to bed?"

"Thinking about it. My eyelids are so tired. I was hoping we could cuddle for a bit."

"Can you give me fifteen minutes? I should be able to wrap everything up by then.

"Sure. You know where I'll be."

He was just about done when he heard a 'ding' on his phone. He saw a text message from an unrecognized number. All it said was 'hi.'"

"Who is this," he replied.

"It's Jordan. I activated your phone today. I just wanted to say thank you."

"You're welcome. How did you get my number?"

"I don't understand technology too well, but the guy at the phone store said your phone was dual-SIM, whatever that means. He replaced one of the cards so I could activate my phone number, but left the other in the phone. It had your contact information. It has a bunch of others, too. But I promise I won't access them or text anyone. This was a big gesture on your part, and I don't want to violate your privacy."

"I'm just glad you're back on your feet."

"Me too. And so is my mom. Anyway, I just wanted to say thanks. Have a good night."

"You too, Jordan. Good night."

Murphy departed for the bedroom, hoping Mollie hadn't yet fallen asleep in the time it took to have a short conversation with Jordan.

"I saved you a spot," she said, as she patted a part of the mattress next to her.

"Excellent. Scoot over, chica."

Chapter Thirty-Five

"Robbie, my man! What's shaking, amigo?" It was just another day at Sterling Investments, with each employee doing their thing.

"Hey Joe. I've got something for you," he said, as he handed him a red folder.

"Ooh, look at this. My man in Compliance walked into my office with a red folder. What did you stumble across today?"

"An interesting scenario. I was comparing the online quarterly investor statements to the paper copies that get sent out, and I came across an inconsistency."

"An inconsistency, interesting. And in the compliance world, that's a…"

"Red flag."

"Tell me more," replied Joe. "I'm all ears."

Robbie opened the folder and handed him a piece of paper. "This is a screen print from an online statement. It shows a quarterly gain of 2.75%. But when you look at the statement that was sent to the investor, it only shows the gain as 2.5%."

"That's certainly an inconsistency. How much was in the account?"

"Two mil."

"So, that quarter point was worth…" Joe paused to do a little math in his head. "Five thousand dollars!"

"I know it doesn't sound like much…"

"The dollar value doesn't matter, you know that, Robbie. Every customer is treated the same here at Sterling. Are you saying the broker shaved a quarter point off of the earnings?"

"I'm not yet in a position to draw that conclusion."

"Did you see where it went? Was it transferred to another account?"

"I need to do some more research. But it was a red flag, for sure, and it's an investor account for one of your new guys, which is why I wanted to bring it to your attention."

"Who's the rep?"

"It's Murphy."

"Murphy… wow. That's… well, that certainly is interesting."

"Do you want me to keep digging?"

"No. This is great. I'm glad you came to me. You're right. He's one of my guys, and I'm responsible for all of the activities that go on under me. Let me take care of this. Thank you. This is great work."

"Thank you, Joe."

Joe then took the conversation to a more personal level.

"How are the wedding plans coming along?"

"Great. I can't wait."

"When's the big day?"

"In two weeks."

"Wow, that's pretty soon. Sounds like there may be a bachelor party in your future."

"Can't wait for that, either. We're headed to Miami this weekend."

"This weekend? Well, have fun. And be safe."

"Thanks, Joe."

"You know what? Do me a favor... on your way out, leave your hotel information with Amy. I'd like to make sure there's a nice bottle waiting for you guys to help kick off your weekend."

"Oh, that's not necessary."

"I know, but that's how I roll. Please, let me do this. You work hard. I'd like to help you celebrate."

"Sure. Thanks. You're the best, Joe."

"Keep doing what you're doing, Robbie. Keep this firm on the up and up."

Robbie offered a thumbs up and, as instructed, paid his assistant, Amy, a visit on his way out. Barely five minutes had passed when Joe made his way over to Amy's desk.

"Did Robbie leave you his hotel information?"

"Yeah. It's right here," she replied, as she held up a small piece of note paper. "He told me you were going to arrange for some liquid festiveness in his room to help with the celebration. That's nice of you. Want me to make the call?"

"Nope," he said, as he snatched the paper from her hands. "I'll take care of this one myself. Thanks."

From closed doors, Joe made the call, just not the call he said he was going to make.

"Heather? It's Joe. What's shakin'?"

"Joe... baby... it's been forever. How you been? You looking for some company this weekend?"

"Not me. But I do need a favor. From one of your girls. Maybe two. In Miami. You name the price."

"Wow! You got a whale in town? Someone you're trying to show a good time?"

"Let's just say I'm involved in a game of chess and I need to make a strategic move. Can you help me?"

"Haven't I always been there for you, baby?"

"You have. Can I stop by later and give you the details?

"I look forward to it. Bye, Joe."

Chapter Thirty-Six

"I'm concerned about Murphy."

Mollie was tucked into a booth with Melissa at a local diner, eating a Cobb Salad and sipping unsweetened iced tea.

"What's wrong?"

"I'm so embarrassed to say this, but..."

"What? Mollie... we've been friends forever. You can tell me anything."

"I think he might be having some sort of breakdown."

"No! Why do you think that?"

Mollie looked around to ensure nobody else was listening. "He's been having these episodes."

"What type of episodes?"

"Sleepwalking."

"Really? Well... that's harmless, isn't it?"

"Normally, yes. But the other night..." Mollie paused. She wasn't sure she wanted to verbalize her concerns, as that would make them more real. But she was with her best friend, someone she could share anything with.

"What happened the other night?"

"He was in the pool."

"What?!"

"By himself. At four o'clock in the morning."

"Oh my God! Are you serious?"

Mollie nodded.

"How do you know he was sleeping?"

Once again, Mollie paused, unsure how to put the situation into words. "He's walked in the past. Usually when he's stressed. And he says the craziest things."

"Is he stressed now?"

"I believe he is. With the new job. He's still trying to get a handle on all of his new accountabilities."

"Did he say anything?"

"When?"

"When you saw him in the pool?"

"I'm going to ask that you keep this between us."

"Of course."

"He's been having hallucinations."

"No!"

"Yes."

"What kind of hallucinations?"

"He claims he's seen a ghost."

"A ghost?"

"And the ghost is the one who convinced him to get into the pool."

"Mollie, I am so sorry."

"I'm freaking out. His sleepwalking has never really bothered me in the past. It's always been somewhat entertaining, to some degree. He always carries on some type of nonsensical conversation, I laugh, and we normally go back to bed together. But this past episode…"

"He's putting himself in jeopardy."

"Exactly."

"Mollie, I'm going to say something right now. Take a moment and let it sink in. Don't judge, just listen."

"Okay."

"Two words. Baker Act."

"What will that do?"

"He'll freak out, for sure, but it gives you up to seventy-two hours to have him tested for mental illness."

"Holy shit! Mental illness? He'll go ballistic!"

"Mollie... you said he's seeing ghosts. And he's swimming in the middle of the night. That's not normal."

"I know, I know."

"Having him Baker Acted gives you an opportunity to have some psychological testing performed."

"I can't believe we're having this conversation."

"I know, but... Look. I'm just mentioning it as an option. Maybe you can to talk to him about it. He can go in voluntarily."

"Yeah, right. Like that's going to happen."

"Or... it can be involuntarily."

"How does that work?"

"If necessary, my co-workers can help."

"How, exactly?"

"They're police officers. They can take Murphy into custody and deliver him to a psychiatric facility for examination."

"Take him into custody? Are you serious?!"

"I'm just laying out options. Obviously, an involuntary route is a last resort. But if he's going into the pool while he's asleep, that's a problem that needs to be solved. He can hurt himself. If you leave this issue unattended, who knows what he could do next. Driving while asleep? Mollie, you've got to take control of this situation."

"I agree."

"Do you want me and Jeff to come over for some type of intervention?"

Mollie just sat there, stunned, and a lone tear drifted down her cheek. Melissa reached across the table and grabbed her hands. "Mollie? We can help."

"I know. This is just so surreal. I can't believe we're actually having this conversation."

"I'm here for you. You know that."

Mollie smiled, as her lone tear was joined by others. "I know. Thank you."

"He needs help."

"I know. You're right. We need to have a talk."

"You tell me when, and Jeff and I will come over. You don't have to do this alone."

Chapter Thirty-Seven

While Mollie was enjoying lunch with a friend, Murphy was back at the office. He sauntered over to Joe's office to update him on the recent trip.

"Hey boss."

"There he is. How did the solo gig to ATL go?"

"From a business perspective, it went great. From a travel perspective, not so much."

"What happened on the trip?"

"Flight was cancelled."

"Did it have anything to do with that freak snowstorm up north?"

"Yeah. And it was the last flight of the night."

"Ahh... So, you..."

"Slept at the airport."

"I hate to say it, but it happens. It's not fun. The chairs are fine when you're waiting for a flight, but they're super uncomfortable to sleep in. The last time that happened to me, my ass hurt for days."

"Yeah. But the gig went great."

"You know me, Murph. One question. Did it close?"

Murphy nodded his head.

"Attaboy! Nice work."

"They're faxing over the paperwork later today."

Joe noticed he had left the red folder, the one containing Murphy's account, on top of his desk. He wasn't yet prepared to discuss it. So, in the middle of their banter, he nonchalantly grabbed it and slid it into the drawer. Murphy pretended not to notice. But, he did.

"When you left, you mentioned there were forty-one employees at the company you were visiting. How many of them have a retirement account that we'd be taking over?"

"Twenty."

"I never understood why every single person doesn't have one, especially when the employer matches employee contributions. They're leaving free money on the table. That's so dumb."

"I was going to say *fiscally irresponsible*, but yeah, not a smart move on their part. But they did ask me to come back when we're ready to launch and help roll it out. They're hoping I can convince the remainder to sign on."

"A worthwhile trip. When it's ready to go, just book it. I don't need to be there for that."

"Starting to trust me a little more?"

"I never doubted your abilities, Murph. Our partnership was at Sterling's request. But I will admit, when compared to the other investment managers, you do seem to achieve better results. I'm proud of you. Keep up the good work!"

"Thanks. I appreciate the compliment."

"Speaking of Sterling, he wants us to hit the road again. He forwarded me a whale that he wants to pitch."

"And you want to partner with me?"

"At his request, my man. He's got a lot of confidence in you. Let's hook up later in the week and we'll map out a game plan."

Murphy gave him a thumbs-up and went back to his desk feeling like a million bucks. The red folder thing was interesting. But he didn't put too much thought into it. If it had anything to do with him, he was sure Joe would have mentioned it. He decided to call it an early day, as he had a surprise planned for Mollie.

Chapter Thirty-Eight

"Hello?" asked Mollie, as she walked through the front door to what appeared to be an empty home.

"Hey. Welcome home. How was your day?" Murphy asked, as he peeked his head out of the kitchen.

"It was great. I had lunch and a shopping day with Mel. Never mind that," she said, while inhaling deeply through her nose. "What's that heavenly smell?"

"Dinner."

"What did you bring in?"

"You mean, what did I cook?"

"You cooked? In the house? Your cooking never smells this good."

"I know, right?"

"Seriously. It smells delicious. How did you...?"

"I overheard some of the girls talking about their favorite recipes at work. I never had much luck in the kitchen, but I wanted to cook for you, you know, make something special. They convinced me that with the right recipe and step-by-step instructions, there's no reason I couldn't pull it off."

"I'm both intrigued and impressed. You didn't use any garlic, did you?"

"You're safe. One clove, minced."

"Okay, well at least that's a step in the right direction. So, what's on the menu for tonight?"

"Blackened fish tacos."

"Wow, your first gig back in the kitchen and you chose seafood? You're brave."

"Fresh-caught Mahi Mahi, coated with a spicy seasoning, a blend of smoked paprika, brown sugar, garlic, cumin, chili powder, salt and black pepper, pan-fried until lightly charred, served in a corn tortilla with all the fixings, drizzled with a creamy avocado-cilantro-lime sauce on top."

"Who are you and what did you do with my husband? The bravest I've seen you get in the past was adding both ham *and* cheese to an omelet."

"That's because I was always nervous. I've screwed up so many meals, I just gave up."

"Remember when you flipped a pancake into the ceiling fan?"

"That was pretty funny."

"And the time you started a small fire when you microwaved ramen noodles but forgot to put water in the bowl?"

"Another classic."

"How about when you dropped a knife while cooking naked and almost cut off your...."

Murphy interrupted her before she could finish. "If I were to put together a kitchen highlight reel, all of those would definitely be on it. But after giving it some thought, I've concluded that failure is not a destination, it's just part of the journey. Sometimes you have to get back on the horse after you fall off."

"Well, if it tastes as good as it smells, we may have to change our house rules and let you back in the kitchen on a more regular basis."

"That's what I'm hoping. Dinner will be ready in about ten minutes. I'm just finishing up the avocado sauce."

"I'm starving. And as much as I like to laugh at your kitchen mishaps, I'm excited you're showing a renewed interest. I can't wait to taste tonight's entrée."

"Prepare to be wowed."

Chapter Thirty-Nine

A few days later.

"Dinner's good," commented Murphy. He had a couple of great days in the kitchen, and then allowed Mollie to take over the reins for this evening.

Mollie appeared to be distracted, as her husband's question was met with silence.

"Hon?"

"Yeah?"

"Dinner's delicious."

"Oh, thank you."

"Is everything okay?"

"Mm hmm."

"You just seem… someplace else."

"I'm sorry. It's one of those days. I have a lot on my mind."

"Anything you want to talk about?"

"No."

Something was up. "Her demeanor is never like this," he thought to himself. "She's always happy." Clearly, something was bothering her. But she was tight-lipped, so the reason remained a mystery. But not for long.

Knock, knock.

"I'll get it," announced Mollie.

Murphy was a little surprised. She got up quickly, almost as if she was expecting someone.

"Oh my gosh.... Hey guys. Murph... Jeff and Melissa are here."

Murphy swallowed his food, wiped his mouth with a napkin and made his way to the living room to greet his unannounced guests.

"What are you two up to?" he asked.

"We were just kind of driving around. Mel commented that we hadn't seen you and Mollie in a while. We figured we'd pop by and say hi."

"Your timing is great. We just finished dinner. Come on in, I'll put a pot of coffee up."

Murphy departed for the kitchen and as such, was unaware of the awkward stares and whispers from the other room. A few minutes later, he returned with the coffee, as well as a homemade lemon bar that Mollie had made earlier in the day. It was odd that she chose this random weekday to bake. It was almost as if she expected company. But Murphy brushed it off as a coincidence.

"How have you all been?"

"Great."

"Jeff... you acclimating okay with your new police department?"

"I am. They're a great crew over there."

There was an odd silence between questions, almost as if the conversation was being forced. He would now find out why.

"So, listen... Murph... we'd like to talk to you."

"Sure."

"We... we weren't just driving around. This visit was planned."

"Why the secrecy?"

154

Jeff looked at Mollie, who looked at Melissa, who was staring at the floor, as she couldn't look Murphy in the eyes.

"Guys... what's going on? Mollie?"

They weren't sure who should chime in first, so Jeff decided to take the lead.

"We're concerned."

"About what?"

"You."

"Mollie, what the hell is he talking about?"

His own wife offered no reply... just a single tear that ran down her face.

"Wait a minute. I think I understand. Okay, yeah... Mollie and I are involved in a really weird argument right now. That has to be it. Is that it?"

Mollie nodded.

"Jeff, I gotta tell you, buddy, it's the most incredible thing. Mollie doesn't believe me, but I swear to God this is true. Our house is haunted. Well, let me rephrase that. Haunted sounds scary. But there's this ghost that comes out at night."

"Mollie told us."

"His name is Pablo. He's the nicest guy."

"Murph... He's not real."

"He is. Trust me."

"You've been sleepwalking," shouted Mollie.

Normally, personal issues such as that were kept private, between a husband and wife. But this wasn't a normal situation.

"Yes. I've been sleepwalking," he admitted. "I know."

"How do you know, Murph?" asked Mollie.

"Because you told me. But this is different."

"Why? Because you have perfect recollection?"

"Well, yeah."

"It's in your head."

"I can't believe we're having this conversation in front of our friends."

"They're just as concerned as I am."

"We are," confirmed Jeff.

"So, you don't believe me, either?"

"Ghosts? Come on, listen to yourself."

"Mel? You too?"

The room quickly became silent.

"Boy, some friends I have."

"Our friendship is why we're here."

"Is that a fact?!"

"Mollie feels... well, we all feel... you should have some tests done."

"Tests?"

"Yeah. Just to make sure everything's okay, you know, health wise."

"Holy shit! You all think I'm crazy!"

"No, we don't."

"This is an intervention, isn't it? Mollie... you staged a fucking intervention?!? I tell you about an incredible experience and this is how you pay me back? By telling me I'm crazy?"

"We'd like you to come with us, Murph," added Jeff.

"Oh, I don't think so," Murphy replied, adamantly.

"The wheels are already in motion. It would be easier on everyone if you come voluntarily."

"Fuck you!"

Jeff anticipated the evening would play out this way, and was fully prepared. He pressed a bunch of keys on his phone and sent a quick text message. Within thirty seconds, four uniformed officers from the police department entered the home.

"This is unbelievable."

"It would be best if you didn't put up a fight. Someone might get hurt."

Mollie began crying and ran into the kitchen. Melissa followed to comfort her.

"I'm being arrested because I believe in ghosts?"

"You're not being arrested."

"So, what would you call it?"

"You'll be held for up to seventy-two hours so some medical tests can be performed."

"You're Baker Acting me?!? Are you serious?!"

"Murph… this is at Mollie's request. Come on, buddy. I'm certain there's nothing wrong with you."

"As am I," he replied angrily.

"That being said, we have to face a few facts, the most serious of which is you're swimming while you're asleep. You're putting your life in danger over some weird episodes of somnambulism."

"That's a big word for a little man like you."

"You're swimming while you're sleeping," he repeated. "Who knows what's next? Driving? We should wait until you put other lives at risk? This is a medical condition. It can be treated. Successfully."

Murphy was silent.

"I need you to come with us," concluded Jeff.

"I don't have a choice, do I?" he asked, as he glared at the officers.

"No, not really."

"What about my job?"

"We'll offer some type of excuse… maybe a death in the family. Mollie can call your employer tomorrow."

Murphy glanced towards the kitchen. He felt betrayed by the one who was supposed to love him more than life itself. What he couldn't see is that was the exact reason she felt compelled to do this.

"Fine. For the record, I'm not going willingly."

"Understood."

Murphy saw Mollie's head peeking out of the kitchen and shot her an angry glare that said something to the effect of "you bitch." He then got up and left with Jeff and the four uniformed officers. The search for mental illness had begun.

Chapter Forty

"All the tests came back negative," said the doctor.

"So, no brain tumor?" asked Mollie.

"No," he confirmed. "His brain activity appears to be normal and healthy."

"Well, that's a relief. But it still doesn't shine any light on the issue." Mollie played the role of a very concerned spouse, and for good reason.

"I have one more thought. I'd like you to see a colleague of mine. How open are you to hypnotherapy?"

"Hypnosis? You mean putting him into a deep sleep? I guess that's harmless. What do you think it will show?"

"I don't know. But if everything he's experiencing is on a subconscious level, it might give us a chance to tap into that unconsciousness. It may help, it may not. But I'm thinking with a licensed hypnotherapist, it can potentially be productive."

"You're the doctor. If you think it'll help, sure. Can I be in there with him?"

"That's up to the specialist, but I'm assuming they would prefer you not be. It might make him nervous, you know, like he's performing for you. And that anxiety may prevent him from achieving the level of relaxation he needs to achieve. But they'll likely have a video camera running, so you can hear and see the entire process."

Mollie went to visit her husband, who was now at the tail end of his seventy-hour stay.

"Can I come in?"

"Suit yourself," he replied, briskly.

"Still mad?"

He looked at her with a glare so chilly it could frost a window.

"I'm sorry," she countered. "I am. But I felt like I had no choice."

"Did any results come back yet?"

"Yeah. You're fine."

"Well zippity-fucking-doo-da. How about that?"

"They do think you have a possible sleep disorder."

"Who's they?"

"A number of doctors."

"I sleep fine."

"Not enough."

"Like most of society."

"And you walk."

"It's rare, Mollie."

"It's becoming less rare."

"Says you!"

"Yes, says me. Honey, why can't you accept that there's something wrong with you?"

"That's not it. If there was, I would seek treatment immediately. You know how serious I take my health."

"I do, too. Which is why I did this."

"I can't stay mad at you, Mollie. You're my best friend. But you're not my favorite person right now."

"I understand. There is a bright side to all of this."

"Yeah? What's that?"

"I got you out of work for a few days. A chance to do nothing but rest."

"It did feel good to sleep. I haven't slept all night in like, a month."

"So, listen, even though all tests showed nothing, thank God, they had a suggestion that I think we should try."

"This ought to be good."

"Hypnosis."

"You're out of your mind."

"No, seriously. They feel what you're encountering may be driven by dreams, or something else in your subconscious. They feel this might allow us to pull back the curtain and tap into that state of mind."

Murphy sat there, fuming. He knew what he saw. He knew what was going on every night. Even if she didn't believe him. But he had to cooperate, to some degree, if they were going to maintain their marital bond.

"Hon?"

"Yeah."

"Yeah, what? You'll do it?"

"Will it help you sleep easier at night?"

"I believe so. I'd like to seek help down any avenue that might offer it."

"Fine. Set it up. Just get me out of here. I'm way behind at work and have a lot of catching up to do."

"Maybe work is a trigger? You know, subconsciously."

At this point he decided to tell her whatever she wanted to hear, even though he didn't agree with it.

"Possibly."

Chapter Forty-One

"So, Mollie, do you have any questions before I get started?"

"This is all so new to me. I guess... I don't know. While he's in a trance, are you just going to tell him that ghosts aren't real?"

"I can try, but the reality is that's not how hypnosis works. It's not effective in changing someone's beliefs. We're going to start a conversation, I'll ask him some simple questions, then some leading questions, and we'll see where it takes us."

"Okay."

"Are you interested in adding any post-hypnotic suggestions?"

"What's that?"

"Well... the short version is that it's a suggestion made to a patient in a hypnotic state that generates a suggested behavior or a predicted outcome. For example, we do it often with people who want to quit smoking. We suggest to them, while they are under a trance, that the taste of a cigarette is putrid, causing them to dislike the habit."

"Ooooh, that's a good idea. Can we do that?"

"Is your husband a heavy smoker?"

"No. To be honest, he's been a non-smoker his whole life. But lately... when he sees these hallucinations, he has three cigarettes each night."

"That doesn't sound like much of a habit."

"Oh, I know. It's not. But he won't admit to it. He's convinced it's the spirit who is doing the smoking, not him."

"Ahhh. I gotcha. He's seeing things that aren't real, so he's projecting this, too. I think that's a good idea. A post-hypnotic suggestion may actually work. It certainly couldn't hurt to try."

"Exactly."

"Okay. Good. I'll work that in. Anything else?"

"Can we do something fun?"

"What do you mean?"

"I've seen hypnotists at comedy clubs, where they make people say or do crazy things. Like, if someone mentions the word 'dog' they start barking."

"As a licensed professional, I'd prefer to limit this session to content that would complement what we're trying to accomplish. This process needs to be taken seriously. It's not a lounge act."

Mollie gave him a sad face. "I know. I'm sorry. I'm just a little anxious over this whole ordeal."

"I'll tell you what... if you come up with something harmless, I'll consider it."

"Well," countered Mollie, "how about this? If he sees me stir a cup of coffee with a cinnamon stick, he'll kiss me on the cheek and say 'I love you.'"

"That's sweet."

"Harmless enough?"

"I think so. Okay. I'm going to head in and get started, and I'll come get you once I'm done."

"Thank you."

The therapist entered the studio, a darkened and soundproofed room designed to assist with relaxation.

"Murphy, are you ready to get started," he said in a low, slow, soothing voice.

"Sure. Knock yourself out."

"Great. I want you to listen to my voice. I'm going to speak very calmly. You are in a very safe place. All is calm here. All is safe. Peace is all around you. Let yourself sink into the chair as you relax. Your eyes may feel heavy, let your body react naturally. Let your muscles relax. Relax your toes. Relax your feet. Listen to my voice, feel the calm atmosphere in the room. You are in complete control. You're just listening to my voice. Breathe deeply... good. Now exhale. Do it again. We're just going to focus on breathing. I want you to look at that poster on the wall. Good. Let your eyes relax. They're growing heavy. You're very relaxed right now. As I continue to speak, the relaxed feeling will get stronger and stronger. You're drifting into a deep and peaceful state."

The therapist continued with his process, all designed to get the participant to relax, which is necessary to bring about a state of deep trance.

"Murphy, you're now in a very deep trance. You feel very safe and relaxed. Let's start with a couple of simple questions. What was the last homemade meal you had?"

"Enchiladas."

"Do you like enchiladas?"

"I love when Mollie cooks Mexican meals. She's a great cook. But..."

"But what?"

164

"Between you and I, she's a little heavy-handed with the cilantro."

The doctor laughed. "Noted. Some people don't like Mexican food. They have trouble digesting it, and an unsettled stomach can keep them up at night. Do you sleep well at night?"

"Usually."

"Do you walk in your sleep?"

"I've been told."

"Who told you?"

"Mollie."

"Do you remember anything when you sleepwalk?"

"Sometimes, but not normally."

"So, you rely on Mollie to tell you what you've done or what you've said when you walk in your sleep?"

"Yes."

"What are some of the things you've done or said in your sleep?"

"She told me it looks as if I'm wide awake. Sometimes I go into the kitchen for a drink. If she sees me there, she'll talk to me."

"Do you talk back?"

"Yes. But she says most times it's mixed up words and I make no sense."

"Okay, good. Tell me, who's Joe?"

"A guy I work with. He's one of my bosses."

"Do you like him?"

"We get along."

"That's not what I asked. Do you like him?"

"I guess. He's greedy and arrogant and seems a bit shady. Those aren't personality traits I normally mesh with. But he's my mentor and he's really smart, so I'm trying to be flexible. I'm hoping I can learn a lot from him, and he can help me be successful in my job."

"Do you like your job?"

"It's a little stressful, but very rewarding."

"Rewarding in what way?"

"Financially. I earn based upon my efforts. The harder I work, the more I make."

"Is that why it's stressful?"

"Absolutely."

"I'll bet you meet a lot of people in your job."

"I do. Between cold calls, office visits and on-site presentations, I meet someone new every day. It's actually one of the things I like most about it."

"So, you like meeting new people."

"Yes."

"Who's Pablo?"

"He's a friend."

"Is he someone you met through your job?"

"No. He's a... neighbor."

"How long have you known him?"

"Only a couple of months. But we've become close."

"How often do you see him?"

"Almost every night. But he's kind of a loner. He's only comfortable visiting me."

"He's never met Mollie?"

"No. Mollie wants to meet him, but whenever she waits up for him, he never shows up."

"What do you and Pablo talk about?"

"It's random. All sorts of things."

"Have you ever gone out with Pablo?"

"No. We just talk... In my backyard. He likes it there."

"Have you ever done any other activity with Pablo?"

"We play poker occasionally."

"Who's a better player?"

"We're about the same."

"Okay, what else? Have you ever gone out to dinner with him?"

"No. But I've had dessert with him."

"Have you?"

"He likes ice cream."

"Interesting. Good, okay, have you ever gone to the movies with him?"

"No."

"Have you ever gone swimming with him?"

"Yeah."

"Does he like to swim?"

"Yeah. That's where he shares things."

"What things?"

"Things he can't put into words."

"I'm not sure I understand."

"Neither do I. It's hard to explain."

The therapist then asked the question that he was leading up to. "Is he real?"

Murphy was silent.

"Murphy, is he a real person?"

Still, no answer.

"Okay," continued the doctor, "let's try this from another angle. Do you believe unicorns exist?"

Murphy laughed. "No. Of course not."

"What about Santa Claus?"

"As a symbol of Christmas, yes. As a living, breathing person... No."

"Do you believe there's an afterlife?"

"A question that millions have pondered, yet nobody can answer."

"Well, a belief is just that. You don't need proof to believe in something. For example, many people believe in ghosts. Do you believe in ghosts?"

There was a short silence in the room.

"Murphy? Do you..."

"Pablo's a ghost," he replied, interrupting the doctor in mid-sentence.

The doctor repeated the statement like a trained parrot. "Pablo's a ghost?"

"Yes."

"The same person who visits you each night?"

"Yes."

"The one you play poker with?"

"Yes."

"Interesting." The doctor was thrilled, as he was hoping this admission would eventually come out, and it finally did. "But let me ask again. Is he real?"

It was a question that remained unanswered.

After a few more questions, he brought the session to a close. "Okay, Murphy. I'm going to count to five, and when we get to five, you will feel wide awake, fully alert, and completely refreshed. One, you're slowly becoming more aware of your surroundings. Two, you feel very rested. You know where you are and you feel good. Three, you're almost ready to open your eyes. Four, you feel good, you're getting more awake. Five."

"How did I do?"

"You did great. How do you feel?"

"Amazing, actually. I feel like I've slept an entire night. How long was I out?"

"You weren't really out. You were in a state of trance, a state of deep relaxation. But you feel good?"

"I feel great."

"Good. I'm going to let Mollie know we're done, and I'll bring her back here."

Chapter Forty-Two

"Well, that was interesting." The hypnotherapist took pages and pages of notes, all of which were designed not only to diagnose, but also to keep Mollie in the loop. She was all ears and anxiously awaited the feedback.

"What did he say?"

"He... believes... he has befriended a ghost."

"Really?" Mollie asked incredulously.

"Yes. He's convinced. But when I pressed him to confirm if he was real or not, he couldn't... or wouldn't... answer."

"So... your conclusion is...?"

"Based on everything we know to date, I can't help but agree with you. I think this Pablo person is a figment of his imagination. Let's put our belief in ghosts aside for now. For me, the most telling fact is that he's the only one who can see him. That being said, my best educated guess is that he's sleepwalking. You said he's done it in the past."

"Yes. More times than I can count."

"And he's confirmed that, as well. It's not a new thing for him."

"Well, seeing hallucinations is."

"Sure, but sleepwalking isn't. And speaking nonsensical words isn't either. He told me that too. The hallucinations could just be his dreams produced during his deep sleep."

"Is there anything I can do?"

"We have to get to the root cause."

"He usually walks in his sleep when he's stressed."

"He did say he was under pressure at work, and it was creating a certain degree of stress."

"He started a new job a few months ago. He was promoted and got a lot of new responsibilities. He's in sales."

"He told me that. I agree, that is a high-pressure job, always chasing quotas. It's quite possible that's the catalyst."

"I can't ask him to quit his job. He has a family to support."

"I'm not suggesting that. But for now, I think the next step might be to consult with a doctor who specializes in sleep disorders. They are best-suited to help unlock the mystery."

"Sleep disorders?"

"The medical term for sleepwalking is 'somnambulism.' It involves getting up and walking around in a state of sleep. I have to be honest, it's interesting that it's even happening."

"Why do you say that?"

"Well, it's normally more common in children than adults. In fact, it's usually outgrown by the teen years. Not that it's unheard of. It's just less common. In any event, isolated incidents often don't signal any serious problems or require treatment, however..."

"However?"

"It if occurs with any regularity, it may suggest an underlying sleep disorder. I think you need to consult with a specialist."

"Thank you. I will. Any other words of advice or encouragement?"

The doctor smiled. "Lighten up on the cilantro."

Chapter Forty-Three

After days of test after test, doctors came to the same conclusion that Murphy knew all along. There was nothing wrong with him. Yes, he was a sleepwalker. Yes, he's had some recent episodes after a four-year sleepwalking sabbatical. Yes, they were brought on by stress. But it didn't change his beliefs. He and Mollie were still at odds over his late-night visions.

"The doctors said the ghost was a figment of your imagination," she would argue. But she wasn't there. She never sat with him. She never spoke to him. She hadn't interacted the same way he had, each and every night. Could she be right? Maybe. But it all felt so real. He decided he needed to keep the visits under wraps. That was the only way to keep Mollie off his back. Clearly, this was driving a wedge between them. If he didn't mention ghosts, then she wouldn't freak out as often. He decided the best approach, for the time being, was to get back into the routine she was used to. So, he went back to work.

"Sorry for your loss, buddy."

"Oh, that's right," he thought to himself. "Everyone thinks someone in my family died and I had to fly out for a funeral. Well, I guess it's better for them to think that than to know the truth. I couldn't imagine the hell I would go through if everyone knew I was Baker Acted and my own wife thinks I have a screw loose."

Murphy got back into his groove and started with some personal administrative tasks. He was a detail-oriented guy. Some would argue a bit too much. But in the financial industry, with so much money passing hands, and all of it under the microscope of the SEC, he felt there was no detail too small. Plus, since his efforts and results had a direct correlation to his income, he wanted to make sure he was paid every penny he was entitled to. No more, no less. That being said, part of his routine involved reviewing his accounts and reconciling his compensation. He normally never found any issues. Until today.

In his previous role as a broker, just a couple of months earlier, he opened an account for a wealthy surgeon. But for some reason, he could not account for the commission associated with that investor. It made no sense, as the firm rarely made mistakes when it came to commissions.

When he brought the investor up on the computer, he noticed the letter "C" next to the account number.

"Ahh. That's it," he said to himself. "It's in Compliance for some reason. Okay, let's start there."

"Can I help you?" asked the young lady.

"Hi. I'm Murphy."

"Hi Murphy. I'm Lisa. How can I help you?"

"I'm trying to locate an investor file, and it's showing that it's here in Compliance."

Compliance played a large role in the firm, and the folders were color-coded based on the severity of the issue at hand. Yellow was a simple issue. Orange was a little more severe. Red was the most severe. Lisa began looking through her pile of yellow and orange folders, but couldn't locate it."

"I'm sorry. It's not here."

"How is that possible? The computer says it's here."

"Well, we're only allowed to share information on the yellow and orange accounts. And that's not one of them."

"You have other colors?" he asked.

"Oh yeah," she replied. "We have red ones, too. Those are for more serious issues. But Robbie handles all those."

"Can I talk to him?"

"Unfortunately, no. He no longer works here."

"Really?"

"Yeah. It's strange. He's getting married in a few weeks. But he quit right after his bachelor party."

"That's odd. Did he give a reason?"

"No."

"And nobody else can tell me if my investor was red-flagged?"

"Not yet."

"That's a problem, don't you think?"

"Yeah. We know. Mr. Sterling is working on upgrading everyone's access so we can all get to that information."

"Oh, okay. How long will that take?"

"We should be up and running by tomorrow."

"Excellent. I'll pop back then. Thank you, Lisa. You've been a great help."

Murphy left the Compliance office a bit concerned. He then played a few recent events in his head. "The psychic said a big problem would arise at work. She said the same thing to Mollie, and that it involved someone named Robbie, who, oddly enough, was no longer employed at the firm. He had an account that might be red-flagged. And Joe tried to hide a red folder from me."

All of these puzzle pieces seemed unrelated. But were they? There was only one way to find out.

Chapter Forty-Four

Murphy called his wife to let her know he had to work late.

"How late?" she asked.

"I'm not sure."

"Is everything okay?"

"Oh, yeah. Everything is fine. I just have to do some follow-up work with a client. It shouldn't take too long, it's just, well, he doesn't free up for a couple of hours, so I can't even begin until then."

"I'll keep dinner warm for you."

"Thanks. Love you. I'll call you when I'm on the way home."

It was a partial truth. It was true that he couldn't start until the end of the work day. But it wasn't because that's when the client freed up. It's because that's when Joe went home. He didn't want to do it, but felt he had no choice. He had to get into Joe's desk and see that red flag for himself. He had to know if it was his client, and if so, why it was flagged.

Amy, who sat outside of his office, was the first to leave at 5:30pm. Joe, who normally worked late, had concert tickets that evening and left shortly after her at 6pm. Murphy waited for a few others on the floor to depart for the evening, as he wanted as few witnesses as possible.

When they met earlier that day, Joe had put the folder into his bottom left drawer, so that's where he started. He lifted a few of the contents, and sure enough, there it was. Upon opening the folder, he discovered that it was, in fact, for his investor. For some reason, an account he opened, and he's opened hundreds of them, was red-flagged. Now he had to figure out why.

Murphy began thumbing through the pages, but couldn't make any sense, as there were no notes. There were only two pages in there, and they appeared to be identical. Both pages listed the name, address, account details and capital gains during the most recent fiscal quarter. It was only when he started going over each page, dollar-by-dollar, did the issue make itself clear. And boy, did it ever.

Chapter Forty-Five

The next day.

"You mother fucker!"

Joe was wondering if Murphy would ever find out. He wasn't aware if he was detail-oriented enough to cross all of his T's and dot all of his I's. Apparently, he was.

"Shut the door," commented Joe, calmly.

Murphy did more than shut it. He slammed it, which forced a picture on the wall to fall and shatter, attracting the attention of everyone on the floor, including Mr. Sterling, who was making his daily rounds.

"Sit down."

"You stole from my customer?!?" shouted Murphy.

"Sit. Down."

"No! You're not controlling this conversation. I am. Top-performer, my ass. You're a fucking thief."

Joe sat there and let Murphy get it all off his chest.

"How long, Joe? How long have you been screwing my clients?"

Joe preferred to remain silent... at least for the time being.

"It is all about the money with you, isn't it? How much is enough?" He repeated his comment again, as he pounded on his desk. "How much?!? I warned you not to fuck with my investors."

"You should sit."

"You're going to jail."

"Sit down!" he shouted, as he lifted up an award on his desk. "Do you remember a couple of months ago, we had a conversation about this?"

"Recognition you likely didn't deserve."

"Maybe. But we were talking about SAT words. Remember? I called this a gimcrack, and you had no idea what that was."

Murphy remained silent, seething.

"It's time to learn a new SAT word. Complicit."

"Come again?"

"Complicit. You know what that means?"

"Yeah. It means involved in wrong-doing."

"Very good. The act that you're accusing me of…"

"Hardly an accusation," he interrupted. "I have proof. You embezzled money from the firm."

"I did. You're right. You're also complicit."

"Bullshit. I am not. I'm honest, I'm ethical…"

"And you're complicit."

"Just because it was my investor doesn't mean…"

Joe cut him off. "You're right. That, by itself, doesn't mean anything. But if you had completed your research before barging in here, you would have learned that the act that you describe was performed on *your* computer."

"What?!?"

"While you were logged in."

"What?!? How the hell…?"

"Let's just say I have many friends. Some inside the company, some outside the company. If this were discovered and investigated, all fingers would point to you, my friend. I guarantee it."

After that terse exchange, Murphy finally sat down.

"Just so you know," Joe continued, "it was discovered."
He opened his drawer and held up the red folder.

"By Robbie in Compliance?" Murphy asked.

"Yep, he was good at his job and did what he was paid
to do. But I took care of the situation. So, your reputation,
and more importantly, your career and your freedom are
left intact. You can breathe easy. Robbie left the
company."

"Was he fired?"

"For what? Doing his job? No, he moved on to greener
pastures. All I can say is, he's not an issue."

"He could still tell Sterling if he chose to."

"He won't. I won't tell you why or how I know, but he
won't. Trust me."

"Trust you?! You're a fucking psycho."

"Yeah, but a rich one. And I'm gonna make you rich,
too."

"I don't want to accumulate wealth this way."

"Stop being so high and mighty. Do you have any idea
how much money we manage? What I took was a grain of
sand on the beach. Besides, I don't think you have much
of a choice, since you work for me. Well, maybe that's a
premature statement. Let's go over your choices, shall
we? You don't like working for this firm anymore, you
can quit. Of course, you can't say why, because it's you
who embezzled money. At least, that's what they
evidence says. Or, you can go to Sterling and rat me out.
But again, once they investigate, well, I hate to sound like
a broken record, but there aren't many ways you can play
your hand. Lastly, you can stay here, and we can do what
we're paid to do: We can make our investors money, and
earn some for ourselves at the same time. Oh, plus the
gimcracks. Let's not forget about those."

"I don't want any part of your get-rich-quick schemes."

"I wasn't suggesting that, nor am I inviting you to participate. You and I are different. I get that. You're young and ambitious. That will certainly pay dividends for you. But I'm blazing my own path. I don't need passengers on my train. But the fact still remains that Sterling wants us together. So, you'll have to come to terms with the fact that I'm an asshole."

"I already have."

"And I'll ask that you keep this conversation to yourself. I have friends, Murph. And I know how to use them."

Chapter Forty-Six

Later that evening.

"You look troubled," commented Pablo.

"There's a problem at work."

"It's with your boss, isn't it?"

"Yeah."

"I thought you two worked it out."

"I think he's just a bad seed. He put me in an impossible situation. Not only that, I can't tell anyone."

"You can tell me."

"I don't think you can help. Not this time."

"Still... it might feel good to share and get it off your chest."

Murphy wasn't convinced but forged ahead anyway. "I'm in trouble. My boss is stealing from the company."

"How does that affect you?" Pablo inquired.

"He's somehow using my computer, my login credentials and my investors."

"Whoa. That's one heck of a trifecta."

"No shit."

"So, he's embezzling money from the firm?"

"Yeah."

"How much?"

"Small amounts... a couple of thousand dollars at a time. He shaves a fraction of a percent from the market gains and alters the investor statements prior to them going out. The numbers themselves are small enough that they typically go unnoticed, or so he hopes."

"Maybe he'll get caught."

"He's already been caught once."

"What happened?"

"One of the guys in Compliance flagged my investor when the quarterly statements were being generated. Joe took it from him, and that was that."

"No follow up?"

"The dude in Compliance just up and quit one day. Joe was able to brush it under the carpet. But he's still doing it. I've checked my accounts. There are inconsistencies everywhere. He's acting like he's untouchable."

"Why can't you turn him in?"

"Didn't you hear what I said? My computer. My login. My fucking investors! Every facet of this crime points to me. It was all part of his design. He's bulletproof."

"You could quit."

"I thought about that. I'm sure that's what he'd like me to do. It probably unnerves him that someone actually knows what's really going on. But this is my dream job. It's a great firm and I've been there for years. I've paid my dues and I'm making a name for myself. Besides... even if I did, that won't exempt me from future punishment. They run audits all the time. I could be working anywhere and they can still come after me. It's a crime. That day would eventually come."

"So... you can't tell Mollie?"

"Are you serious? For starters, she'd freak. I mean, she would totally believe me. But she would insist I go to the police. She wouldn't understand the lengths he's gone through to make himself invisible in this process."

"We can ask for spiritual guidance," said Pablo, as he motioned towards the pool.

Murphy stopped pacing and stood directly in front of the shallow end, his sadness reflected back to him in the water. "I thought about that. If I felt there might possibly be an answer to this, I'd go in, in a heartbeat. But there's literally no road I can take, and I've considered every conceivable option. I just know if I go in, they'll show a picture of me in jail. I just couldn't live with that image ingrained in my mind."

"So, what are you going to do?"

"What can I do? Nothing. I'm going to have to act like everything is normal. I'll go to work and do my job. And he'll continue being a douche. I just have to hope he doesn't get too sloppy or greedy, or it's me who'll pay the ultimate price."

Chapter Forty-Seven

The next day.

"Hi Murphy."

"Hi Mr. Sterling. You wanted to see me?"

"I wanted to say thank you for the thoughtful birthday present. That certainly was creative. How did you know I was into coffee?"

"Amy told me."

"Ahh… Amy. Well, she offered some wise advice. Thank you."

"You're welcome."

"Grab the door. Please, sit."

"Uh oh," he thought to himself. "I think he knows." He was hoping to avoid a confrontation with his CEO, as he presently had no way to defend himself from the evidence. Luckily for him, Sterling had a different conversation in mind.

"I wanted to congratulate you on your performance this quarter. You seem to be catching on quickly in the retirement investment arena. I saw you made the top ten percent of earners."

"Well, I was a broker, for you, previously."

"And a good one."

"Thank you, sir. This was just a matter of understanding the new products inside and out."

"I noticed you and Joe having an argument the other day. At least, it looked like an argument. And quite honestly, it sounded like one, too."

Murphy chose his words carefully. "It was just a disagreement. It was nothing, really."

"You two seem to have a lot of those. And if I can be blunt, that looked like it was more than a disagreement. I know I only got a short glance, but you appeared pretty angry. Are you having issues working with him?"

"No sir, not at all."

"Because I can't help but think part of your success is based on that mentorship."

Once again, Murphy's thoughts raced through his mind. *"Did he just say that? My success is because I'm fucking good at what I do. And he's a goddam thief."* But of course, he was nothing if not always politically correct. "I believe that to be true, sir, to some degree."

"I put you two together because I wanted his success to rub off on you. He's going places. And if you play your cards right, you will be too."

"He's a unique character, Mr. Sterling. His work ethic takes a little getting used to."

"I don't really care how you do it, Murphy. Just work it out."

"Yes sir."

"If I see you two arguing in an office, I'm sure other people do, too. We have a culture here, one of teamwork and collaboration. We can't live up to our vision if my star players are at odds with each other. So, work it out."

"Yes sir."

"How is your lovely bride?"

"Mollie? She's great."

"Please send her my regards. She's an important part of your success, too."

"Don't I know it," he confirmed.

"Thanks again for the coffee card. It truly was very thoughtful. I'm looking forward to visiting the café. Thanks for stopping in."

"Thank you for your time, Mr. Sterling."

Chapter Forty-Eight

3am.

"I've been meaning to tell you," began Pablo, "this is a nice house. I like this outside area in the back. It's very comfortable."

"Thank you."

"It's big. Are you and Mollie the only ones who live here?"

"Yeah. We bought it because we thought it would be a great home to raise a family in. But the family thing hasn't quite worked out yet."

"Why?"

"We're not sure. We're just having trouble conceiving."

"Would you like to find out why?"

"We've tried. We've both been to doctors. We know there's nothing wrong on my end. And the tests on Mollie have been inconclusive."

He knew Murphy heard the question, but didn't process it as he intended. So, he asked one more time, enunciating each word individually. "Would... you... like... to... find... out... why?"

It finally clicked, and Murphy replied with genuine curiosity. "You know why?"

"No, but the spirits do."

Murphy was intrigued. He normally never believed in any of that spirit mumbo jumbo, but then again, here he was, eating ice cream with a ghost.

"Okay. Tell me. Consult the spirits. Why can't we get pregnant?"

"I can't just ask them. It's more complicated than that. But we can discover the answer together."

"I don't understand."

Pablo motioned towards the pool.

"Oh, hell no! Are you out of your freaking ghost mind? Absolutely not!"

"There are unexplained forces all around us, every minute of every day. I thought I've proven that?"

"Yeah, well, the last time I got in the pool with you, you sent me to a coffee shop where I got assaulted. Then I was Baker Acted and had to undergo days of primping, prodding and testing in the search for mental illness."

"Did they find anything?"

"Of course not. But it was fucking humiliating. Not only that, everyone now thinks I'm crazy! Swimming with you is not good for my health."

"The answers are out there. You just have to be open to them. You've already proven you're the type of soul who can not only receive, but decipher those messages."

Murphy sat there with conviction. Yet he was also despondent at the big picture. He and Mollie wanted to start a family so bad. Bad enough, that he gave Pablo's suggestion a final thought. If he could find an answer, a legitimate answer, the risk would be worth the reward.

"Jesus, if she catches me in the pool again, I'm beyond screwed."

"So, you'll try it?"

A moment of silence passed between them.

"Fine," he replied, as he pulled off his shirt. "But this better work."

The two slowly walked into the pool, until Pablo quickly stopped and got out.

"Where are you going?"

"They told me I needed to finish my milk first."

"Are you fucking kidding me?"

"Nope. That's what they said."

"Why?"

"Murphy, at some point you'll need to learn, when the universe tells you to do something, you don't ask why."

"You're a strange ghost. Get your poker-playing, milk-drinking, ice-cream-eating ass in here."

Pablo returned and the two faced each other, standing waist-high in the shallow end of the pool.

"Okay," said Pablo. "Hold my hands and close your eyes." They went through the motions and assumed the position. "*O, forti universum, ut vocarent te: ostende nobis, ut nos videre non possunt.*"

A few bubbles began to emerge around them. And then, on the movie screen in their heads, they see a young girl, seventeen, maybe eighteen years old, and she's standing behind a counter.

"That's the girl at the coffee shop. I met her last time I went in."

"She has the answer."

"A girl I barely know? At the café?"

"Yes. They say the truth lies with coffee."

"That is, by far, the most ludicrous thing I've ever heard."

"The universe is never wrong."

"In this case, they are. They have to be. There's no way."

191

"Why is it so hard to believe?"

"Are you listening to yourself? Seriously... listen to what you're saying... listen to what *they're* saying."

Pablo remained adamant and unphased. "I have."

Chapter Forty-Nine

Back at the café.

"Well, this is starting to become a habit."

Murphy was convinced this trip was for naught, and it truly was a waste of time. But he was certain his ghost guest would be upset if he didn't at least follow through. So here he was.

"What can I say. Nobody brews a better cup of Joe."

"You say that," replied Jordan. "But you get the same, generic, boring cup of coffee every time."

"Do I?"

"Yes. I remember all of my customers' orders. I've got a great memory."

"Okay, make mine from memory."

"That's easy. One cup, medium roast, shot of sugar-free vanilla syrup, non-fat milk instead of cream."

"Wow," he replied. "You are good."

"Told ya," she added, with a smile.

Murphy took a sip and confirmed it was as good as all the others he had ordered in the past. "Mmm."

"It's a good thing you're not trying to get pregnant," she said, which caused him to choke on his coffee.

"What did you say?"

"Sorry... I didn't mean to make you choke. You're a guy. Guys can't get pregnant. I was making a joke."

"Yeah. Okay. Ha ha. But what did you mean?"

Jordan was trying to keep the banter light and fluffy, but Murphy, with his serious tone, was intent on hearing more.

"You always get fat-free milk. Fat can actually play a role in the ability to get pregnant."

"I call bullshit on that."

"Well, then you're going to have to take it up with Harvard University."

"Huh?"

"I only know this because I just did a paper for school. There was a Harvard medical study which concluded that low-fat dairy foods could increase the risk of infertility, whereas high-fat dairy foods may decrease it."

"I'm sorry, could you say that last sentence again? Slowly, please, so my brain has a chance to process it."

"High-fat dairy foods may decrease the risk of infertility. It has something to do with the fat in dairy. Don't know what it is, but it seems to play a role."

"Dairy. Fat. Fertility. Harvard. Holy shit!"

"Are you okay?"

"Do you have a take-out cup?"

"Leaving so soon?"

"Um, yeah. I gotta go. Great cup of java, by the way," he added as he turned to leave.

"Mix it up next time, Murph," she shouted, as he was still within earshot. "Go with the cream."

Murphy went back to his office and instead of working and preparing for his next presentation, he spent the remainder of the afternoon on the internet. And sure enough, there were a myriad of articles spouting legitimate research making the same exact claim. He printed off dozens of articles to take home to his bride.

194

She may think he's crazy for swimming with a ghost, but the universe just delivered, and in a big way.

Chapter Fifty

"We need to talk."

"Murphy… I hate when you start a conversation that way. It's exhausting," replied Mollie.

"It's not about what you think it is. No ghosts. No sleepwalking. No more fighting. Truce?"

"Truce. What would you like to talk about?"

"It's about our baby-making activities. I'd like to try something."

"What? Here? On the kitchen table? We've already done that. Twice."

"No, I'm serious."

"I couldn't tell with that goofy smile on your face."

"It's not about where we do it or how we do it. It's a little more scientific than that."

"I'm listening."

"There's just one caveat."

"What's that?"

"You have to forsake some of your nutritional values. At least temporarily."

"Oh, jeez. Here we go. Did you read some outrageous claim online? Like if I eat squid dipped in chocolate, I'll get pregnant? Hon, everything you read on the internet isn't true."

"You're right," Murphy countered, as he opened his folder. "But some of it is. Especially when it's based on research supported by Harvard University, The University of Rochester and the U.S. National Library of Medicine.

"So, I don't have to eat candy-coated grasshoppers because some ancient Indian savant saved the population of his village that way?"

"Nope. Dairy fat."

"Dairy fat? We've known our whole lives that too much fat isn't good for us. That's why we buy…"

"Skim milk," he interrupted. "Yeah, I know. And fat-free ice cream for dessert. And sugar-free creamer for our coffee. But check this out."

Murphy pulled out article after article, all spouting research supporting the same conclusion. Foods low in dairy fat could increase infertility.

"Are you serious?" she asked.

"It's not one source, or two, or three. I've got a stack of research here that all says the same thing. So?"

Mollie was quiet, reading an article in one hand, and holding two more in the other. "Harvard University?" she asked.

"It's worth a shot, don't you think?"

"Well, yeah! Absolutely. When do we start?"

"Right now. I stopped at the store on the way home. Milk and ice cream and creamer, the way nature intended it."

"How did you stumble across this?"

He decided to tell the truth. Well, some of it. He left out the part about swimming with a ghost. The last time that happened, it didn't end well. "It was a random comment someone made at that coffee house in Ybor."

"You've been spending a lot of time there lately."

197

He nipped this potential argument in the bud with a short reply. "It may have paid off, don't you think? Right place, right time."

"Give me a glass of milk. And go get naked."

"I don't think it works that fast."

"Doesn't matter," she said with a smile. "This is the most encouraging news I've heard in a long time. We're celebrating!"

Chapter Fifty-One

Murphy went back down to the coffee shop again after work. Though Jordan didn't know anything about his issues with his wife, they were invigorated at the random nugget she threw at them. They had been trying for years, and they now had renewed faith. He wanted to share his joy, and at a minimum, thank her.

"One coffee, cream, two sugars, please." Murphy placed his order with a random employee, looking around to see where his new friend was. He noticed the place was quieter than normal. There were plenty of people there, but they were all in a lull, kind of like they were depressed.

"Will that be all?"

"Yeah. Hey, where's Jordan?"

"Jordan?"

"Yeah. She usually works right about now."

"You didn't hear?"

"Hear what?"

"She's kind of missing."

"What do you mean, kind of?"

"We don't know much. Her mom called here yesterday, trying to locate her. Apparently, she couldn't get in touch with her. She never showed up for work. She called the school and discovered she wasn't at her last class, either."

"Nobody knows where she is?"

"No. Her mom filled out a Missing Person report. We're waiting for some flyers to post around town."

"Oh my God, are you serious?"

"Unfortunately."

Murphy turned and sat on one of the vacant couches, deep in thought. "Missing. Wow. That's horrible."

Since she was the only reason he was there, he finished his coffee and left.

Chapter Fifty-Two

2:23am.

"How was your day?" asked Pablo.

"Not so good. I went down to the café. Everyone there was sad."

"Sad? Why?"

"The girl who always helps me... She's missing."

"What do you mean, missing?"

"Missing. Nobody knows where she is. A Missing Person report was filed with the police. The staff is getting ready to put flyers with her face on it all over the streets of Ybor."

"Oh my God, are you serious?"

"Yeah."

"I'm so sorry. You always lit up when you spoke about her."

"She was very spunky. A ball of energy. She was just, well... she was such a sweet girl."

"Was? Why would you speak of her in the past tense?"

"These things rarely end well."

Pablo became silent and lit a cigarette. He was about halfway through when his eyes opened wide.

"Are you okay?"

"This is it!"

"This is what?"

"The person I'm supposed to help. This is the one!"

"A missing girl? You think this is why you're haunting my backyard?"

"It has to be."

"You don't know anything about her circumstances. Maybe she ran away."

"She didn't run away. She was met with darkness."

"That's one heck of a conclusion you drew, without knowing any details."

"I can feel it in my bones."

"If that's true, then how do you know she's still alive?"

"Come with me," Pablo said, as he made a motion toward the pool.

"I don't know about this."

"The truth is out there. We need to see it if we're going to figure out how to help her. Come on!"

The two parked themselves in the shallow end, with the hope of discovering any information about her disappearance. One Latin phrase later, with water bubbling beneath them, they waited impatiently. And then, an image finally came through. Thought they didn't physically see her, they saw all the makings of an evil act. Rope, duct tape, towels and chloroform. They both came to the same conclusion. If this young girl was, in fact, missing, then she was abducted.

"Well, now we know. It's time to take action," said Pablo.

"How do you intend to find her, Mr. I-Can't-Leave-The-Premises?"

"With your help, Mr. Ghost-Ambassador."

"Sorry, man. This is way, way out of my league. I think we just let the police do their thing."

"I don't know that they can. That's why it was assigned to a spirit."

"You really think this is why you're here?"

"She's young, she's bright, she has her entire life in front of her. Yes, I do."

"It's great that you know. But… I don't think I can help you."

"Why?"

"Because I'm not a detective. I'm not a cop. I have no authority to do anything."

"But you have investigative skills."

"Do I?" he laughed.

"You figured out your boss was stealing once you put all the pieces together."

"This is different."

"Is it? I'm stuck in limbo until I can help someone. When we asked for hints, they showed us the café. You've been there a dozen times trying to gain some information."

"Yeah, and I got none. I just met a nice girl. Who's now missing."

"You're wrong. I'll prove it to you. You discovered someone's apartment was broken into. Then another. Then another. That's quite a coincidence."

"It's probably just a bad part of town."

"Signs, Murphy. Not coincidence. Signs. Did the victims have anything in common?"

"Besides being robbed?"

"Yes. Any common traits? Gender? Age? Think…"

"Well, when you put it that way, yeah. They were all women. Single women."

"How do you know they were single?"

"No ring on their fingers."

"You're happily married. Why do you check out everyone's ring finger?"

"Bad habit."

"What else?"

"They were all young. Mid-twenties or younger."

"Is it possible they have that in common because that's the demographic that hangs out there?"

"No… I've seen all age ranges. In fact, I've seen all body types and hair colors, as well. Now that I'm thinking about it, each victim was slender and had dark hair."

Pablo repeated what Murphy had said thus far. "All young women. All single. All dark hair. All slender. All congregate at the same café."

"It's still nothing more than a coincidence. What we really need are fingerprints." And then it dawned on him. "You know what? The police have the prints from each break-in. And they match each other. Which means the same perp broke into all of the apartments."

"How do you know?"

"Random dinner conversation. A couple of our friends are in law enforcement."

"So, one person broke into three apartments, and all three belonged to women who fit a similar physical profile, who spend their free time at the same place. That's huge. And you still think it's a coincidence?"

Murphy shrugged his shoulders. "The problem is, those prints aren't in their searchable database."

"Which means what?"

"This person doesn't have a record. So, it really could be anyone."

"Yes and no. I mean, yeah, we don't know who it is, but I would bet my soul the person who's involved is a patron from the café as well. How else can three people of a similar profile, from the same location, be picked at random? You're a numbers guy. What are the odds?"

"I would say pretty high."

"Sounds like we narrowed it down quite a bit."

"So, what do we do? Do we just present our information to the police? Maybe they can fingerprint all café visitors over the next couple of weeks."

"I don't think we have a couple of weeks. We probably don't even have a couple of days. With each passing day, the chances of us finding her alive decline. I hate to resort to appearances and first impressions, but did you meet anyone sketchy, maybe a little off kilter, someone you think could be capable of this?"

Murphy thought for a moment. "You know what... there was this one guy. He was studying a law book. I spoke with him one day and he made the weirdest comment."

"Which was?"

"I asked 'why law?' He said 'I'd like to be able to defend myself when I'm arrested.' Or something to that effect."

"That is odd. It's like he's already committed a crime."

"That's kind of what I was thinking when he said it, so I distanced myself from him pretty quickly."

"He could be our guy. Can you tell your police officer friend about him? Maybe they can tail him."

"They won't listen to me."

"Then you can follow him."

"I'm not going to follow him. Pablo, this is a job for law enforcement. Let them do it."

"You and I both know they won't do it with the expediency it requires. Tell me this, has this person been there every time you've been there?"

"Every time. He's there, literally, every day."
"So, he's a regular. You should go back. Tomorrow."
"And?"
"If he's there, get his prints."
"How the hell am I supposed to do that?"

Chapter Fifty-Three

The next night.

"I can't fucking believe that spook talked me into this." It was just after midnight, and Murphy, dressed in old jeans and a t-shirt, was standing inside the dumpster located just outside of the café. The last time he went dumpster diving was a decade ago, when Mollie accidentally threw away some savings bonds, mistaking them for junk mail.

He was surrounded by a mountain of black garbage bags, a collection of café waste for the day. "Where the hell do I start?"

It was a monumental task, to say the least. He now knew where the expression 'looking for a needle in a haystack' came from. He was looking for one random cup in a sea of waste, one in which the name 'Jay' was written on the side in marker. He began by opening one bag, and pulling out its contents, one cup at a time.

Eventually he found his groove and was making progress, reviewing the waste from one end of the dumpster and tossing it to the other end once it was reviewed. He wondered if this episode was as disgusting as his Jell-O wrestling match during Homecoming Weekend in college. "This is so fucking gross," he said to himself, confirming that this task easily took first place.

His gross journey took a turn for the worse when he heard someone bang on the side of the receptacle. "Uh oh."

He peeked his head out from behind a pile of sifted garbage, and was met with an ominous voice.

"You're about to have a really bad night."

As fate would have it, it was the police, and Murphy was quickly arrested for trespassing.

One hour later, sitting in a holding cell, he was given a glimmer of hope from the officer on duty. "Time for your phone call. You only get one, so make it count."

Chapter Fifty-Four

"Murphy, what the hell is going on?"

"Thanks for coming down, Jeff."

"Seriously, man. Why am I here? It's the middle of the night, for crying out loud!"

"You're the only person I know who could probably get me out of this."

"I did. Tampa PD owed me a favor. They saw you had no previous record and they released you to me."

"Thanks. Melissa doesn't know you're here, does she?"

"Of course, she does, you nutjob! You woke us both up at 2am. Why didn't you call Mollie?"

"I can't. It's... it's complicated."

"This doesn't have anything to do with all those medical tests you took, does it? You're not sleepwalking right now, are you?"

"Yeah, Jeff. I'm sleepwalking right now," he replied sarcastically.

"Sorry, it just... you've been going through some weird changes and it has us all freaked out."

"I'm fine. I promise. But now that Mel knows I'm here, I need a favor."

"I just pulled your ass out of jail, amigo. You've used up your goodwill."

"Not from you. From her."

"From my wife?"

Murphy reached into his pocket and pulled out a crumpled, used coffee cup. He was careful to handle it from the edge and not touch the middle.

"Don't even fucking tell me…"

"I need her to run prints on these."

"Murph…."

"Jeff… You read about the missing girl from Ybor, right?"

"Yeah. So?"

"She had her apartment broken into a couple of weeks ago."

"And you know this, how?"

"That was the one you brought me in for questioning. Remember?"

"That's an interesting coincidence."

"No shit. But here's where it gets strange. There were three apartments broken into over the course of two months."

"And…?"

"And I think it's the same guy. And, whoever did those crimes kidnapped her."

"This is getting way out of your league, brother."

"I know. That's why you're here. Just hear me out. Three burglaries, each victim was a single female. Each one is a frequent customer at the same coffee shop in Ybor."

"Probably a coincidence."

"I don't know about that. I'm got a really strange vibe from one of the other patrons. He made a really weird comment, something a normal person wouldn't say."

"Murph… come on, man."

"Jeff, I need you to take me seriously."

"It's just… in my line of work, that's called a hunch."

"So?"

"Hunches don't always pan out."

"But sometimes they do. I need Melissa to check the prints, and then cross index them with the prints associated with the burglaries."

"And if it's not him?"

"Then we're in no worse shape than we are right now. But if it is… you'll have a chance to rescue her. And solve the burglaries, of course. You've got to help me!"

Jeff took possession of the coffee cup, making sure not to press his prints where others should be. "I don't know about this."

"If you're wondering, the Fourth Amendment doesn't apply here."

"Are you trying to school me in the law?"

"Just trying to remove any doubt you might have. Once the garbage is in a receptacle ready for pick-up, there's no right to privacy."

"I know what the Fourth Amendment is."

"Then you know this can't be categorized as an unreasonable search. Please… just give it to Mel and let her do her thing."

"And Mollie?"

"She can't know about this. We've been having a few issues. I'll just sneak back into the house before she wakes up."

"She's not the only one who's worried about you."

"I know. Trust me… I know."

"Where's your car?"

"Back at the café."

211

"Okay. We're going to drive over there, I'm going to drop you off, and you, my friend, are heading straight home. Got it?"

"Yes sir!"

"You're goddamn right, yes sir. Get your trespassing ass in the car."

Chapter Fifty-Five

Next day at Sterling Investments.

(ring... ring... ring).

"Sterling Investments. This is Murphy."

"Hey, Murph. It's Jeff."

"Any word?"

"Melissa fast-tracked it and ran it through IAFIS."

"And?"

"No match."

"What? That can't be right."

"She said she ran it twice and got the same result both times. Whoever you think did this, didn't."

"Goddammit!"

"I'm sorry."

"It's okay. Thanks for getting the cup over to her. It meant a lot to me."

"I'm here for you. But I'll say it again... I am worried about you. Please let the police do their job."

"Yeah, yeah."

"Murphy, I'm serious. This is a dangerous business. You have no idea where she is or who has her, or if she's even alive. Not to mention, you don't even know who she is."

Murphy held the phone, but remained silent.

"Let the police do their job."

"Thanks, Jeff. Please thank Melissa for me, too."

"I will. Now go home. And spend some quality time with your beautiful wife."

"I will. I'm going to call her right now."

Murphy hung up the phone and immediately called Mollie. "Hey, hon."

"Who's this?"

"What do you mean, who's this?"

"I thought it might be my husband, but I forgot what he sounds like since he's travelling all the time," she replied.

"I know. I'm sorry. I'll make it up to you. I have one appointment after work, but I'll be home around 8pm or 9pm."

"So... no dinner together tonight?"

He heard the disappointment in her voice and recognized that his path was starting to affect their marital bond. Only he had the ability to fix that. So, he tried.

"How about I try to move my appointment up, and I'll pick up some dinner on the way home. That way, you don't have to cook."

"I would love that!"

"Okay, let's shoot for 7pm."

"Great. It's a date. Love you. Can't wait for big, big hugs."

"Me too."

Murphy continued on with his day, doing his best to not cross paths with Joe. Though they still had some upcoming trips together, he was one gigantic distraction, and he needed to focus. He had lied once more to his bride. He had no appointment. He was going back to the café. Even though he struck out on the finger prints, he knew the person he sought was somehow connected to that place. Three break-ins and a kidnapping, all associated with people who spent their time there. It was too much to be a coincidence.

Chapter Fifty-Six

"We're going to miss you!"

Murphy had entered the café and walked right into a party. A going-away party, for one of the staff. It was a bittersweet affair, for the joy of moving on to bigger and better adventures was overshadowed by the fact that one of their own was still missing. He stopped prior to the counter and began staring at one of the missing persons posters that was hanging within the establishment.

"Can I get you a drink?" someone asked.

"Who, me?" asked Murphy.

"Sure. You're a regular. I've seen you here plenty of times. Free coffee drinks to celebrate Matt's departure."

"Which one's Matt?"

The worker pointed to a young man, who appeared in his twenties, standing over by one of the couches. He was working the room, hugging and saying goodbye to the customers. He was a popular employee who had earned Employee-of-the-Month at least twice over the past year. Murphy strolled over with his free coffee to say his goodbyes and offer his well wishes.

"Where you headed?" he asked.

"Somewhere. Anywhere. I'm really not sure where."

"That's one hell of a plan."

"I'm going to stay with family up north for a little while. Just temporary, you know, until I figure things out."

"Well, I don't know you, but have a safe trip," Murphy commented, as he reached out to shake his hand.

"Thanks!"

Murphy continued to walk around the café, looking closely at each person. Whether they were in a chair, on a couch, or in the bathroom, he made sure he was aware of every single person in the joint. He was searching for clues, still convinced the answer to the puzzle and the safe return of the missing girl, had to be right in front of his nose. But he just couldn't see it. After about an hour, he decided to head home. The person he loved most in the world was waiting for him.

Chapter Fifty-Seven

Though he was physically exhausted, he had to stay up. He had to provide an update to Pablo. He was hoping for better news, but unfortunately, it wasn't the case.

Pablo lit his first cigarette of the night. "You don't look happy," he said, as he exhaled a puff of smoke. "Couldn't find his cup to check for prints?"

"Actually, I did find his cup."

"And?"

"And then I got arrested for trespassing."

"Jesus! Murphy, I'm so sorry."

"It's okay. My best friend is a police officer. He was able to get me off with no charges filed."

"A lucky break."

"Yeah, well, that was the only lucky break."

"What do you mean?"

"They scanned the fingerprints and confirmed the creepy student had nothing to do with the burglaries."

"Dammit! I really thought we had him. Are you sure he's not our guy?"

"Yeah. I'm sure."

"So, we're back at square one."

"I don't know that we can solve this."

"Don't give up on me."

"I have no other information. Not a shred of an idea of who it could be or where we should look. I even went back to the café tonight to physically look at every single person in the place. I was hoping something would jump out. The fact that all of the burglaries were tied to single girls who frequented the same coffee café is too much of a coincidence to ignore. I just... Someone there has to know something. I know it. I'm just... I'm lost. I've got nothing."

"You're convinced someone there is involved?"

"Yeah. Aren't you?"

"I am. I just wanted to make sure you and I were both on the same page."

Pablo then held up his left hand and positioned his fingers into a peace sign.

"What are you doing?"

"Have you ever heard that when you get older, you begin to forget things?"

"Yeah. So?"

"As you age, memory is typically one of the first things to go."

"I'm not sure what you're getting at."

"It's not like that with ghosts."

"What do you mean?"

"Memory's not an issue. I remember everything about my life, even from when I was a child."

"You weren't old when you died."

"When you're a spirit, your entity is your best self. It's when you looked your best and felt your best. Even when older people pass away, their entities remember everything. We have the ability to watch our memories, any memories, over and over again."

"So?"

"You have memories of the café tonight. You didn't see anything that stood out. Maybe I can."

"I don't understand."

"Raise your right hand and hold up a peace sign."

"You're freaking me out, man."

"I'm going to tap into your memory while it's still fresh."

Murphy squinted with doubt. "And how are you going to do that?"

"Two fingers. Lay your tips on top of mine. I'll be able to see everything that you've seen. Maybe something will stand out, something you didn't think was important."

"Probably because it wasn't important."

"Two sets of eyes are better than one. Come on, amigo. Do this with me. And close your eyes. We can do this journey together.

Murphy was no longer surprised at what ghosts can do, as he had already witnessed things impossible for any human. He held up his peace sign and pressed his fingers against his friend's. They both closed their eyes and began to recount his entire evening.

"There's a party," confirmed Pablo.

"Yeah. An employee was leaving. They were bidding him farewell."

"And there are 'missing person' posters all over."

"Well, she's still missing."

"I see about thirty folks. You did a good job checking them all out."

"Yeah, but I didn't see anything unusual."

"That guy carrying out the garbage looks scary. What's his story?"

"That's Vic. He just started there last month. He just got out on parole."

"Parole?"

"I know what you're thinking, but you can't judge everyone based on first impressions. He's actually a really nice guy."

"Now you're talking with a young kid. Who is this?"

With his eyes closed, Murphy watched the scene like he was at a theater. "That's Matt. He's the one who's leaving."

Pablo paused to listen to the conversation, word-for-word. He witnessed the handshake, and then watched as Murphy headed over to the restroom. "And that's it?"

"Yeah. I tried circling the area, but came up empty-handed. Again."

"We're running out of time. She can be anywhere. We have no way of knowing where she is. Time is of the essence, and we have nothing," said Pablo.

The two sat there for a few moments, deep in thought.

"Actually," began Murphy. "We have a little more than nothing. We have something nobody else has."

"What's that?"

He got up, pulled off his shirt, and made tracks for the shallow end. "A way to connect with people who *do* know. What are you waiting for? Get your spooky ass in the pool."

"I like the way you think, amigo."

The two return to the pool one last time and assume the position.

"Okay," said Murphy. "Show me."

Pablo did his part and summoned for help. "*O, forti universum, ut vocarent te: ostende nobis, ut nos videre non possunt.*"

Bubbles began to rise to the surface as they awaited some type of message. They needed a clue… any clue… to help find her.

"Here it comes," said Pablo. And then they saw it. "Who's that?"

Murphy was shocked. "That's Mollie!"

"Your wife? I don't understand. How is she involved?"

"She's not."

"According to the signs, the clue rests with her."

"That's impossible."

"She's on the phone. Who do you think she's talking to?"

"Probably me," he replied sarcastically. "I'm never home."

And within ten seconds, their message from another dimension went dark.

"That's it," Pablo said. "That's all we're going to get."

Murphy departed the pool slowly, obviously deep in thought, trying to determine how the hell his own wife could provide the answers. Pablo remained behind, opting to stand in the water. "Are you coming out?"

"I think it's time."

"Time for what?"

Pablo nodded to the window to bring attention to the clock in the kitchen. Murphy confirmed the time. "Dammit! You're right. It's 3:56."

"This is on you, Murph. You got this?"

Murphy was silent, again trying to crack this puzzle in the sixty seconds he had left before his partner disappeared once again.

Pablo began to sink into the pool. "Murph… tell me you got this. Please!"

He looked Pablo in the eyes just before he submerged, hoping a moment of clarity would hit him, but it wasn't there. "Sorry, man. I got nothing."

Chapter Fifty-Eight

With no viable clues to follow, Murphy had no choice but to sink back into his normal routine. This particular week, it involved a number of presentations in Georgia and Florida. He would be gone most of the week with Joe.

"What's good here?" Murphy was looking around at the eclectic décor of the evening's restaurant, after a successful round of presentations for two firms in Atlanta.

"Everything," answered Joe.

"I take it you've been here before?"

"Every time I'm in town. The filet is to die for. No fancy seasonings, just some coarse salt and fresh cracked pepper, pan-seared then finished in the oven. They bring it out, sizzling on a five-hundred-degree plate. Every bite melts in your mouth."

"I'm sold. I love a good filet. I'm still trying to perfect them on the grill."

"The key with grilling filets," replied Joe, "is to take them out of the refrigerator about twenty minutes before cooking. Letting the meat come to room temperature allows it to cook more evenly."

"I appreciate the tip."

"Listen… I need to mention something to you. I don't want to make a big deal out of it, but I want to make sure you're aware."

"Shoot."

"Some of your commissions are going to be delayed this month."

"Why would some of my commissions be delayed this month?" he asked in a surprised tone.

"Another three investor files got bounced by Compliance."

Murphy shot him a look of disappointment. "Are you serious? Joe, come on, man. I need those commissions."

"I know, I know. And you'll get them. I promise."

"This is my household's cashflow you're messing with."

"Murph… there's nothing to worry about. I'm the guy that signs off on them. It's all good. I just have to make it look like I've done a little investigation before I approve them."

Murphy just shook his head in disbelief. "This is such bullshit, and you know it."

"Oh, don't give me that crap. I've seen the house you live in. You're doing just fine. An extra week or two on the commission cycle isn't going to put you on the street."

"That's not the point. You're messing with my money."

"I give you my word, you will get every dollar you're entitled to. I promise. The waiter is on his way over. This conversation is now over. So, what do you think? Filet? Or double down with the Surf n' Turf?"

Murphy was infuriated, but there was little he could do. He knew his stellar reputation was now at risk, as his name would keep popping up in Compliance, over-and-over again. Joe had crafted the perfect financial crime. He was now stealing between five and ten-thousand dollars per month. It was pale in comparison to the billion dollars under Sterling's management. But it was still theft. And it still had Murphy's fingerprints all over it.

"Can I get you gentlemen a drink to start off your meal?" asked the server.

"Absolutely. Murph, what would you like to drink?"

Murphy just stared at him, still reeling over the commission comment.

"I said I'd take care of it. What do you want to drink?"

"Scotch, neat, please."

"And you sir," he asked, as he turned his attention to Joe.

"I'll have the same."

Chapter Fifty-Nine

"Are you ready to head out?"

Murphy and Joe wrapped up their evening, maxing out the allowable dollars on their expense account. They successfully mapped out their game plan for the next day's meeting, which they hoped would result in a lucrative contract. That, of course, translated to a healthy commission.

It was a late night. They stayed at the bar until just after 2:00am, long enough so their drinks had metabolized and any buzz they achieved was long gone. They pulled out of their parking space and began the short five-mile drive back to their hotel. They were on the highway when, without any warning, they saw a deer jump out of nowhere and into their path. Joe swerved to avoid her, and in the process, lost control of the vehicle and drove straight into a tree.

Smoke began rising from the hood of the wrecked car. The radio was still playing, but neither of them moved. They were crushed inside the car, each covered in blood from an assortment of injuries. They were both alive, but barely. Murphy glanced at the dashboard and determined the time of the accident. It was 2:14am. That specific time played such a large role over the past few months, but in his present condition, his brain was unable to fully process that fact.

It took a few minutes, but an ambulance finally arrived and took both of them to the hospital, where they were quickly whisked into surgery.

Murphy wanted to talk, but couldn't. All he saw was a team of doctors above him, working to save his life. He tried to move, but was paralyzed, hoping it was just a result of anesthesia. His immediate thought turned to Mollie, his best friend. There was so much more to do together. "Please don't let this be the end," he said to himself.

While on the operating table, his head was tilted slightly to the left, and out of his peripheral view was a clock on the wall. He was forced to stare at it, as he was unable to turn his head. He slowly began to feel weaker and weaker, until everything went dark.

"Paddles! Stat!" shouted the surgeon.

The medical team frantically began the painstaking task of trying to restart his heart, alternating between CPR and delivering shocks through defibrillator paddles. That effort, unfortunately, was futile, as they were unable to revive him after almost ten minutes of activity.

"We can't save him," said one of the doctors. "Call it."

"Cause of death," continued another doctor, "car accident, resulting in blunt trauma to the body and internal bleeding. Time of death... 3:57am."

Chapter Sixty

Knock, knock!

"Hey! Dude! Are you in there?"

No answer.

"Come on, man! Why do you always do this to me? Get your ass up!"

Once more, he pounded on the door.

Bam! Bam! Bam!

Murphy was suddenly awakened from a deep sleep, heart racing, soaked in sweat.

"Let's go, loser! We have to get going!"

He jumped out of bed, tripped over his shoes, and answered the door while still on his knees.

"Whoa. Someone looks like they had a rough night," said Joe.

Murphy stood up and looked around, completely disoriented. He poked his index finger into Joe's chest three times to make sure he was real.

"Are you okay?"

"You're here. I'm here."

"Yeah, and you're being really fucking strange. Get dressed. We gotta go."

"Yeah, okay," he replied, as he wiped the sweat from his forehead. "Let me take a quick shower. I'll meet you downstairs in fifteen minutes."

"Those mojitos really kicked your ass last night, huh?"

"Mojitos... last night... yeah, I guess so. That must be it."

"Seriously, man. Are you okay? You look like you just woke up on another planet."

Murphy closed the door abruptly and ended the conversation.

Joe continued to shout through the door. "Fifteen minutes, Murph! I'll be downstairs in the lobby."

Murphy was completely freaked out. His brain was racing, trying to decipher what just happened, and came to the only logical realization. "A dream. It was just a dream. It had to be a dream..." He grabbed his phone and called his wife. He had to hear her voice. With all that was going on, with all the signs and conversations about the universe this and the universe that... He had to hear her voice. Everything felt so real. He had to make sure it was just a dream.

"Hey baby."

"Well, good morning, sunshine. How did you sleep?"

"Sleep was kind of rough. Joe just pounded on my door and woke me up."

"You were drinking last night, weren't you?"

"Yeah."

"That always puts you into a deep sleep."

That was the confirmation he needed. "You're right. Deep sleep."

"Are you okay?"

"Yeah... I'm fine. Just a bit groggy. I had a funky dream."

"Ha! If you're groggy, it means you had more than a little bit to drink."

"I think you're right."

230

"What did you have?"

"We started with scotch, and... I think we ended with mojitos."

"How many?"

"More than I can remember."

"Will you be okay for your presentation today?"

"I will now. I just needed to hear your voice."

"Aww. That's sweet. I miss you."

"I miss you, too."

"When are you coming home?"

"In a few days. We're driving down the east coast. We have one more presentation in Atlanta later today, then two in Jacksonville the day after that. We have a tentative gig set up in Daytona on Thursday, and I should be home later that night."

"Thursday it is. It's a date."

"Hey..."

"Yeah?"

He wanted to talk more. He wanted to share his experience, as it was quite frightening. And incredibly realistic. She was always the one who could calm him down. But he knew he only had fifteen minutes. And he did achieve his goal: He spoke to his bride, and confirmed whatever he experienced, it was just a nightmare. It was all in his head. And that realization made him wonder... it felt so real, but if that was a dream, how many other things did he experience that could have been dreams? He didn't have much time to ponder, as his ride was waiting downstairs. But that thought would gnaw at him all day.

"Love you."

"Aww. I love you too, baby. Travel safe. Call me later."

"You can count on it."

He hung up the phone and mumbled his way towards the shower. "Goddam mojitos."

Chapter Sixty-One

The last presentation in Atlanta went well, and they were able to get to their next location, Jacksonville, just before dark. After checking in to their hotel, they decided to celebrate the day's efforts with a meal at a local steakhouse.

"This place looks familiar," said Murphy, as he and Joe sat down.

"I come here whenever I'm in town. They make the best filets. Have you had one from here?"

"No. I've never been here."

"Yet you just said it looked familiar."

"Yeah. Strange. I must be thinking of someplace else."

"The prep is so simple. It's just a little coarse salt and cracked pepper. They pan-sear it to lock in the juices and then cook it in the oven and serve it on a five-hundred-degree plate. You've got to have one. I insist."

Murphy replied with two simple words. "Sounds delicious." In his head, he felt a strange sensation, like he already had this conversation.

"Qué quieres beber?" asked Joe.

"What?"

"Qué quieres beber? It means what do you want to drink?"

"Oh... Scotch. Neat. Why were you speaking Spanish?"

"You're going to laugh... I'm trying to help my daughter. She's taking some Spanish classes, so when we talk to each other, we try to keep the conversation in Spanish so she can develop some fluency."

"Oh, that's right. Emily's in college right now. Where does she go?"

"Upstate New York. At Cayuga College, over by the Finger Lakes."

"Is she doing well?"

"Almost straight A's."

"Almost?"

"She got a B in her Journalism class."

"You must be proud."

"Of the grades? Sure. She's doing awesome. But she still manages to keep me up at night."

"Why is that?"

"She met a guy she really likes. Sounds like it might be getting serious." Murphy laughed.

"Nice kid?"

"No idea. I don't know a whole lot about him."

"What's his name?"

"Jonathan. But she calls him Blaze."

"Blaze?"

"His last name is Blazer. But I'm sure it's also because he smokes dope."

"Not everyone who goes to college smokes pot."

"Sure, they do," he answered with confidence.

"You're hysterical. How did they meet?"

"They took an "Intro to the Stock Market" class together and started dating at the end of the semester. And get this… She even talked me into letting her adopt a puppy."

"Really?"

"Yeah, she used her portfolio gains from the class for the adoption fees. She named him Scoop."

"Because…"

"Because she's a journalism major."

"Cute name. well, you're blessed. Mollie and I are still trying. We can't seem to get pregnant."

"Bummer. Listen, I need to switch gears for a sec. I need to mention something to you, something important, so it doesn't come as a surprise."

"Suenas serio."

"What?" said Joe.

"Sorry," Murphy added with a smile. "I wasn't sure how much Spanish you learned. It means 'you sound serious.'"

"Nice one. Yeah, it is. And I hate to say it, but it affects your pay."

"My pay?"

"Yeah."

"Joe…"

"Murph, let me finish. A few of your investor files were bounced over to Compliance."

Murphy sat there with a confused look on his face.

"You seem to be okay with this tidbit of information."

"We've had this conversation before. Yesterday."

"No. No, we haven't. The red flags were just put on my desk today."

"Are you sure?"

"Yeah. Anyway, some of your comp will be delayed by a couple of weeks."

"Because… my files… are in… Compliance?"

235

"Are you okay? You're acting really strange again."

"I'm fine," he replied, but then quickly changed his mind. "No, actually, I'm not. I'm pretty pissed that you're fucking with my compensation."

"I know. And I'm sorry. I couldn't help that. But I promise you will get paid every dollar you're owed."

Murphy's brain alternated between anger and confusion. He was feeling the strangest sensation of déjà vu.

"El servidor viene. Desea pedir?" asked Joe.

Murphy shrugged his shoulders.

"That was good, right? I'm really learning a lot. It means 'the server is coming, are you ready to order?'"

"I feel like I'm getting screwed."

"Then don't get the filet."

"I'm not talking about the filet. I'm talking about you messing with my family's cash flow."

Joe looked over his shoulder to ensure nobody was listening. "What can we do? You want someone else working with Compliance? Do you? We both know what would happen. It has to be me. That guarantees your safety. But I have to make it look like I'm investigating each one, which is why I have to delay the comp."

"Joe..."

"This conversation is now over. I'm only mentioning it to you as a courtesy."

"Again," Murphy thought to himself, for he could swear he had the exact same interaction the previous night.

The remainder of the dinner and subsequent conversation went as they always do. They talked about upcoming presentations, the importance of eye contact, overcoming objections, and ultimately closing the deal.

236

The filets were, of course, delicious, as was the lemon meringue pie they chose for dessert. Joe asked one last question before requesting the check.

"Quieres un trago mas, Pablo?"

Murphy choked on a bite of pie and began coughing. "What did you just say?"

"Quieres un trago mas. Do you want one more drink."

"No... that last word. The name you just said... at the end of your question!"

"Oh... Pablo. I didn't know the Spanish word for Murphy, so I used your middle name. Your wife told me it was Paul. It is Paul, isn't it?"

"You called me Pablo?" he asked, incredulously.

"Yeah, that's... isn't that Paul in Spanish?"

"I'm Pablo!?!"

"Yes. You, my friend, are Pablo."

"I'm Pablo?!" he repeated.

"Are you okay? You look all freaked out, like you saw a ghost or something." He had absolutely no idea of the significance of what he just said. Some would argue it was a coincidence. But for Murphy, it was a sign. The universe was speaking to him. Something big was about to happen.

With no notice, Murphy got up and left for the restroom. He ran the water in the sink and splashed his face. "Okay," he said to himself, "get a hold of yourself. It was a random comment. Purely coincidental." He kept repeating that last statement over and over. But if it were true, why couldn't he stop shaking?

He began to recount all of the events in his head. Bad dream. It's possible it was an alcohol-infused nightmare. But the time of the crash and the time of death were so precise. And those exact times played out over and over again during the past three months. "Did my encounters with Pablo subliminally place these times into my subconsciousness? Or were they all, in fact, related? Pablo said he died in a car crash. And those were his coming and going times at the house each night. Could that be the clue to his mystery... why those times dictated his presence? And Joe, Jesus Christ... he called me Pablo. What the hell are the odds? They'd have to be astronomical. Granted, it was my middle name. But, come on! That's an eerie coincidence. Maybe I am Pablo. Maybe everything I've experienced was a dream. All of it. Maybe Mollie was right. Maybe all of this..."

Murphy paused and stared at himself in the bathroom mirror until he came to the only conclusion he could come to. "Oh my God! I'm going to die tonight."

Chapter Sixty-Two

He continued to splash water on his face and made the decision that no matter what happened, he was not getting in that car with Joe. No. Matter. What.

"Are you okay?" asked Joe. "You kind of freaked out on me." Murphy chose his words carefully, but decided to be direct and to the point.

"I can't go to the next presentation with you. I can't even leave this restaurant with you."

"Is this about your investor accounts? Come on, man, we can easily navigate through those."

"No," he replied adamantly. "That's not it."

"Is everything okay at home?"

"Home? Yeah, home's fine."

"Then what the fuck is your problem?"

"Do you remember when you woke me up this morning?"

"Yeah," he laughed. "You were a mess."

"I had this crazy dream that you and I were driving, and you crashed."

"That is one shitty dream. But it's got no bearing on what we have to get accomplished in the next couple of days."

"Joe... I died."

"That sucks."

"I'm serious. Something bad is going to happen on this trip."

"That's nonsense."

"I'm not going with you."

"I'm sorry, could you repeat that last statement? It sounded like you said you weren't coming with me, but I know I must have heard that wrong."

"No, you heard it correctly. I'm not going with you."

"You and I have had our differences, Murph, but we still have things to do. And we have to do them together."

"You'll have to go on without me."

"You know I'm your boss. You know your job is to do what I say," Joe added, with his voice suddenly getting louder.

"I know."

"If you don't do what I say, you know this can potentially affect your career."

"Are you kidding me? Dreams aside, you've stolen from the company using my name. You've already affected my career!"

The argument was getting heated, and was heard by the few guests who were left in the restaurant. "Get in the car, Murph!"

"I can't."

"Get in the car, or you're fired!"

"You can't do that!"

"Oh, yes I can! Sterling gave me full authority to develop you into a selling machine, and shit-can you if you can't pull the weight!"

"I'm outselling everyone, and you know it!"

"And yet, here we are, stuck at a crossroads. Last chance. You get to decide how it ends."

Murphy thought for a moment, and shared the only decision he felt he could make. "Estas por tu cuenta, amigo."

"Come again?" replied Joe.

"You're on your own, friend."

"And you're fired! Asshole!"

Chapter Sixty-Three

He was sitting in the hotel, shaking. "Get a hold of yourself, man," he said to himself. There was so much racing through his mind. Some folks have a heightened sense of intuition in certain situations. This was different. Murphy knew this was a huge sign, one in which he felt compelled to right some wrongs. If not, the consequences would be devastating. He knew it in his soul. Knowing he no longer had a job, his first course of action was to blast off an email to his now-former CEO. He needed to know the truth. Murphy had to confess what was going on in the firm, right under his nose, and the role that he had inadvertently played. "The buck stops here," he wrote. He decided that although his participation in the embezzlement was not something he planned or executed, he could no longer work there, as his actions would negatively affect the reputation of the brand that the CEO spent years to cultivate. His career was over. He knew it. And he owned it, even though the result might be charges brought against him. It was futile to mention Joe's name. He was the golden child, one who could do no wrong. Sterling had already taken sides with him in previous confrontations. Besides, all evidence pointed to him. If nothing else, the admission would allow Sterling to tighten the reigns so it couldn't happen again. He put careful thought into every word he typed. He read those words over and over, and finally hit 'send.' It was the hardest message he ever had to convey. Now it was time to talk to his wife. This was a huge moment in his life, and he needed to include her. He knew it wouldn't be as easy to compose, as this was incredibly negative and affected them as a family, but he had to face the music. She was his best friend, and best friends share everything, good and bad. They have celebrated the highest of highs together, and have navigated the lowest of lows together.

He punched up his home number from his contact list and called his bride. Unfortunately, she was not there to answer. This was a message he needed to deliver personally, with two live people at the end of each phone, but he couldn't wait. There were too many emotions racing through his mind and he had to get them out. He began babbling and left her a lengthy voice mail message.

"Hey hon... it's me. Listen, when I get home, we need to talk. I've had a crazy day. It's hard for me to explain everything that happened on this trip, but... I did have an epiphany. You were right. About everything. I'm sorry I put you through all this. This whole ghost thing... it was all in my mind. I'm certain of it. I had this strange dream... and then a crazy conversation with Joe... I'll explain it all when I'm home. But the short of it is, I've been having hallucinations. I've been seeing things in my sleep. They seemed so real, but I know now that they weren't. My actions, all of them, were brought on by me following something non-existent from my subconscious. I'm so sorry for putting you through this. I had the weirdest dream."

He continued to ramble for as long as the length of the voice mail would allow. He refrained from telling her about the job and the details of his blowout with Joe. If seeing hallucinations was difficult to talk about, admitting to an illegal act would be harder. That conversation needed to take place face-to-face.

"I will get help. I promise. Whatever it takes. I love you. You are my everything."

He hung up the phone and began to pack his bag. He no longer had any reason to stay. It was time to go home.

Chapter Sixty-Four

Murphy spent most of the day on the road. He was petrified to drive, but took his dream literally. If anything was going to happen, it would have been when he was in the car with Joe, an event he successfully avoided. He was about six hours into the trip when his phone rang.

"Welcome to Tampa," said Mollie.

"How did you know I'm close to home?"

"I'm psychic."

"No, really. I've travelled over four hundred miles today. How did you know I literally just hit the Bay area?"

"I'm a voyeur."

"What does that mean?"

"You remember that program you installed on our phones? The security app. The one that tracks the phone GPS, so we know where each other is at all times. I turned it on earlier and saw you in Georgia, then coming down I-95, then over to I-4…"

"Ahh, gotcha. Yeah, you're right. You are a voyeur. I'm not far."

"I thought the program was broken at first."

"Why did you think that?"

"There were three dots on the map."

"Three?"

245

"Yeah. Two of them were here in town, and then yours, which was hundreds of miles away at the time."

"I don't understand."

"It's okay, hon. It's fine. Probably just glitchy software."

"Yeah, probably."

"So, when do you think you'll be home?"

"With traffic? Probably within the hour."

"Awesome. Love you. Can't wait to see you."

"Me too."

Murphy hung up the phone and turned up the stereo to help pass the time and make traffic more tolerable. And then…

"Wait!" he said to himself. "Three GPS dots? Can't be."

He hastily weaved in and out of traffic so he could pull off and stop the car on the shoulder. He activated the security app to see if he saw the same thing.

"That dot is Mollie… that dot is me… that dot is… No. Fucking. Way."

It wasn't glitchy software. It was the phone he leant to Jordan. And it was not only on, but it was on the move. He quickly tapped a text to Mollie. "Forgot, I have to stop at the office first. Shouldn't take long."

The synapses in his brain were working overload. His heart was pounding. He was ready to write off this episode with the missing girl, as the clue, at the time, was unintelligible. An image of Mollie on the phone? It made no sense. Until this very moment. Jordan had Mollie's old phone. It was not only on the move, he knew exactly where it was, and quite possibly, where she was.

Chapter Sixty-Five

He sat on the side of the road for a few moments, trying desperately to figure out how this was happening. Not fully understanding the technology behind it, he concluded that, even though Jordan activated her own phone number, it was a dual-SIM phone. She only replaced one. It had to be tracking the other. He watched as the dot kept moving.

"On the go, huh? Where you headed, you loser?" He watched as the GPS tracked the phone moving west on the Courtney Campbell Causeway, a 9.9-mile road that connected Tampa's Rocky Point area to eastern Clearwater. Murphy's location on I-275 put him about twenty minutes behind the signal. He got out of the car and retrieved the lug wrench from the trunk. "Might need this," he said to himself. He pulled back into traffic and began weaving in and out of the myriad of cars, trying to make up some time. He wasn't sure of the final location but knew the direction he was headed. That was all he needed for the time being. Thankfully there were no police around, as he was both speeding and driving recklessly in an effort to catch up. He spent the next half hour with his left hand on the steering wheel, right hand holding the illuminated map on the phone. He alternated between eyes on the road and eyes on the phone. It probably wasn't the safest way to drive, but as far as he was concerned, a girl's life was at stake, and he finally had his car within two-hundred yards of the vehicle he sought. He accelerated a bit to close the gap, still not knowing which car he was looking for. As he got closer, he glanced at all of the drivers, then back at the map, then at the drivers again. The map showed Murphy in the left lane, and the car he was looking for was in the middle lane.

"Come on, you son-of-a-bitch. Show yourself." Murphy slowed and then stopped at a traffic light. He was about three cars back from the light. Whatever car he was following had stopped, too. He had it narrowed down to two cars, either the one in the middle lane one car-length in front of him, or the one in the middle lane directly in front of the light. His heart was racing like a thoroughbred racehorse. The light turned green, and he tossed the phone onto the seat. He no longer needed it.

He narrowed his search down to two cars. He slowly drove next to the first car in question, and saw an older woman, maybe in her sixties. He passed her to get to the next one, and while maintaining the proper speed limit, pulled alongside. He first noticed the driver's left arm, hanging out the window. Murphy was temporarily blinded, as the sun's reflection bounced off the driver's watch. And then he saw it. The watch had the face of a Kennedy half-dollar, the same one that had been stolen from Jordan's apartment.

"He's got her phone, he's got her watch… if I were a betting man, I'd say he has her, too," he thought to himself. He pulled up a little more for a fast glimpse, and quickly confirmed what he suspected all along. This person was a regular at the café. Not only that, Murphy was present at his going-away party. It was Matt, who left his job a few days ago. No wonder he replied "anywhere" when asked where he was moving. To him, it didn't matter. He just wanted to be off the grid. He eased off the gas to hang back half a car length to avoid being identified. He had one shot, so he put the wheels in motion and made a quick phone call to his friend.

"Hey Jeff."

"I'm working, man. Is everything okay?"

Murphy knew he couldn't say anything that would provide any value to the situation. Jeff was not only involved in Murphy's involuntary Baker Act, he also had to bail him out of a trespassing charge at two in the morning. Their friendship was a bit strained.

"Yeah. Listen, I just wanted to say you've been a good friend. I'll always remember that."

"Are you okay? You sound really weird."

"You're going to get a call in the next two minutes. It'll all make sense then."

"What? What the hell does that mean? Murphy…"

Murphy then hung up and thought about the next call he was about to make. "Well, there's a good chance I'm going to jail for securities fraud. I might as well go out with a bang."

"9-1-1. What's your emergency?"

Murphy did his best to sound frantic. He spoke fast, and he spoke loudly. "There's been an accident. On Gulf-to-Bay Boulevard in Clearwater. The two drivers are fighting in the middle of the street, blocking all westbound traffic. Please hurry!" And then he hung up. It's showtime.

He dropped back so he was about a car's length behind the suspect. He then moved into the center lane, and then into the right lane. He followed the car for about a half a mile, waiting for the right moment. It had to be calculated, precise, and involve a concrete barrier separating the opposite lane of traffic. And there it was... two hundred yards in front of him. He accelerated slightly, closing the gap until the time was right. With each passing second, he moved a little bit more ahead of the other car, until he was exactly three-quarters of a car length ahead. Once his position was set, he drifted left into the car, forcing him into the left lane and then into the concrete barrier. With Murphy's car wedged in front and traffic now stopped from behind, he had him exactly where he wanted him. He couldn't move.

Murphy jumped out of the car, with crowbar in hand, and went to introduce himself.

"Open the trunk!" he shouted. "Now!"

"What?! No way, you psycho! I can't believe you crashed into my car!"

Murphy then jumped onto the hood and smashed his windshield with one swing. "Open the trunk!" he repeated.

Matt looked around and quickly saw there was no way to escape.

"Fine," he said. "If you're not going to open it for me, I'll do it myself." He attempted to reach into the driver-side window but couldn't locate the latch, so he went for the keys. Matt quickly opened the door, causing the doorframe to hit Murphy in the jaw and slow him down.

Matt immediately noticed that this was a man possessed. He grabbed the keys and crawled over to the other side of the car and quickly exited through the passenger window and into the street. He didn't get far, though, as Murphy tackled him in the middle of the road.

The scene was playing out exactly as predicted. He told the 9-1-1 operator there were two men fighting and blocking traffic. Check. That call would then be dispatched to Jeff, who would arrive on the scene in a matter of minutes. Check. Jeff pulled up just as Murphy put Matt in a headlock, pulling the lug wrench up to his neck to ensure he couldn't go anywhere without crushing his windpipe.

"One last chance before I snap your neck. Give me the keys so I can open the trunk."

"Fuck you!" he shouted, as he then turned his attention to the police. "Help me! Please help! This guy is insane!"

Jeff approached slowly with his hand on his holster. "Murph... what's going on, buddy? You having a bad day?"

"Thank God you're here. He's got her."

"Who?"

"The missing girl from Ybor. He's got her in his trunk!"

"Get this guy off of me!" Matt continued to yell. "He's crazy!"

Traffic was now at a standstill in all directions. Within minutes, more police showed up, and this minor car accident turned into a stand-off.

"Drop the pipe, Murph!"

"Jeff, just open the trunk."

"Let him go, Murph!"

"Did you hear me?! She's in there. I know it!"

"I can't search it. You know that. I don't have a warrant and I don't have probable cause."

"Jeff, if you let him go, she's gonna die!"

"I don't have probable fucking cause!" he shouted. "Drop the wrench, let him go and step away from the car."

"You have to trust me. Come on, man. Don't let my past dictate your present. I'm not crazy."

"Nobody said you were. And this isn't about trust. This is about the law."

"Then arrest him!"

"He didn't do anything, Murph. You're assaulting him. That's the only thing I see."

"Then you're not looking hard enough," Murphy added, as he tightened his grip. "If you don't do something, I will."

"Drop it, Murph. Let's just go down to the station and talk." Like other officers, Jeff now had his gun drawn. Any of them could have ended this situation in two seconds if they chose to.

"He has her."

"There's no proof."

"He robbed her apartment! Come on, man! He's wearing her fucking watch!"

"The burglary has nothing to do with this."

"It has everything to do with this! He stalked her for weeks and waited for the right moment to pounce! He's a predator!"

"Officer," cried the driver, "I've done nothing wrong. This man is a psycho! I was just driving and minding my own business when he rammed my car and smashed my windshield."

"Fuck you, you slimy bastard," replied Murphy as he tightened his grip again. "Open your trunk before I smash your head in!"

"Officer, please help me!"

"What are you going to do, Jeff? Are you gonna shoot me? Me?!?"

"Murph, put it down."

"Listen to me. I'm going to speak very calmly. I know you think I've got a screw loose. With every ounce of my soul, I'm telling you, don't leave without opening the trunk. Arrest me if you want. I'll go willingly. But only after you open the trunk."

"I need a search warrant."

"Follow your gut, Jeff."

"That's not how the law works."

"It does today!" he shouted. "It has to!"

Though there were dozens of people on the scene, the two of them had their eyes locked on each other.

Jeff stuck to the letter of the law, and that involved the Fourth Amendment to the US Constitution. *"The right of the people to be secure in their persons, houses, papers, and effects, against unreasonable searches and seizures, shall not be violated, and no warrants shall issue, but upon probable cause..."*

Murphy was getting nowhere, and he knew it. The situation did not go as it was supposed to. It was one crazy man with a lug wrench against a dozen with guns. Every gun was loaded, and they were all pointed at him. There was no way out. His perfect life was now upside down. He was contemplating his next step, and quickly realized he had none.

Just then, a random butterfly floated in and landed on the wrench, and his mind drifted. He had fond memories of Monarch butterflies, dating all the way back to kindergarten. Every year, Mrs. Dalton, one of his favorite teachers, would create a butterfly garden, starting with dozens of caterpillars. The students were in awe as each

253

caterpillar transformed into a chrysalis. It looked as if nothing happened over the course of the chrysalis phase, which typically lasted ten days. But that couldn't be further from the truth. Those days were a time of rapid change, where each caterpillar underwent a remarkable transformation called metamorphosis, resulting in the birth of a beautiful insect.

He glanced at the trunk that he was desperate to open. He knew in his soul that a beautiful person would emerge from the automotive chrysalis, if given the chance.

Jeff began shouting to his peers, quickly breaking Murphy's concentration. "Mathers, take Winters and set up a crowd line. Make sure no one goes in front of it. Berman, go over to the cross road. Nobody passes through until this is over. Dalton, stay here with me."

"Dalton?" he thought to himself. "Did he just say Dalton? That's quite a coincidence." And just then, the butterfly, which mesmerized him for the past minute, flew away, causing him to ponder one single question. Was that a sign? Or was it *just* a butterfly? After all he had been through, there was only one answer.

He dropped the lug wrench and held up his hands, as if to surrender. He was all in. Matt ran to the other side of the street to put some distance between him and this lunatic.

"It's time, Jordan," Murphy said in a low voice, confident that fate would intervene.

Once the police saw the hostage was freed and the weapon was no longer a threat, two police officers wrestled Murphy to the ground and cuffed his hands behind him. Though he wasn't putting up a fight, they were leaning on him with all their weight, pressing his left cheek into asphalt street.

"Come on, Jordan," he whimpered. "You can do it."

Nobody was paying attention to him now that the scene had been dismantled. The police lifted him to his feet and began walking him to one of the cruisers. Matt was off in a corner giving a statement to another officer.

Murphy continued rambling, a little louder with each statement. "Come on, sweetheart. Tell us you're here and you're okay. We're listening."

"Who the hell are you talking to?" asked one of the officers.

"Now, Jordan!" Murphy shouted, as they opened the door to put him in the back of the vehicle. And before they could, he broke free of their grip and let out one last scream, "NOW, JORDAN! NOW!!!"

That scream was loud enough to command the attention of everyone within a hundred-foot radius. But nothing happened. With tears streaming down his cheeks, he was now forced to face the inevitable. An officer grabbed him by the arm and dragged him back to the cruiser. He pushed him up against the rear of the vehicle and opened the door. Murphy looked down and noticed that the officer dragged his feet into a two-inch deep puddle.

"What's the matter, Harvard? Afraid of ruining your hundred-and-fifty-dollar shoes? I wouldn't worry about that. You won't need them where you're going."

Murphy kept glancing down at the puddle. He was fascinated at this small pool of water sitting in the middle of the road, as if it were placed there for a reason. Within seconds, the water began to soak through his leather shoes and socks, and finally touched his feet.

"You're going to jail, scumbag. Any last words before I take away your freedom?"

It was the last play of the game, two seconds left on the clock, defeat was imminent. Murphy took a deep breath, closed his eyes, and delivered one final Hail Mary.

"*O, forti universum, ut vocarent te: ostende nobis, ut nos videre non possunt.*"

"What the hell did you just say?" asked the officer.

And then they heard it. They all did. A loud *Thump! Thump! Thump!* from the trunk of Matt's car.

Murphy screeched from the rear of the cop car. "There's your probable fucking cause, Jeff! Open the trunk!"

Jeff ran over to the car and leaned over the trunk. "Jordan, is that you? Honey, if you're in there, make some noise."

Thump! Thump! Thump!

The situation took a one-hundred and eighty-degree turn and all eyes were now laser-focused on that trunk.

"Let's get her out of there!" Jeff screamed.

Everybody was awestruck and completely caught up in the moment. It would take less than five seconds for them to realize they handcuffed the wrong person, and the true guilty party was not yet in custody. Unfortunately, it was five seconds too long. In an act of desperation, knowing his monstrous act was about to be revealed, Matt reached down and grabbed a gun out of the closest officer's holster.

"He's got a gun!"

Those four words added more terror onto an already chaotic scene, forcing everyone in the crowd to panic and run in every direction. Matt took advantage of the pandemonium and ducked behind the nearest squad car. Most of the officers ran for cover, except for Jeff. Now that he knew the contents of the trunk, he chose to stand directly in front of it, like a momma bear protecting her cub. He then drew his weapon and aimed it right at the car Matt was hiding behind, hoping to keep him there until the situation could be resolved.

Like a periscope on a submarine, Matt lifted his head up just enough to see through the rear window of the car. He quickly noticed that Murphy was in the back seat of that same vehicle. The two stared at each other, probably thinking of the irony of the situation. Less than two minutes earlier, Murphy had opened a can of whoop ass on him with a lug wrench. Yet now, the tables were turned, and the weapon was upgraded to a gun.

"Nobody has to get hurt," yelled Jeff. "Give up now, and we have some options."

"Options?!" screamed Matt. "What the hell are you talking about?! You know I have none!"

"There are always options. Right now, it's just a kidnapping charge. Pull the trigger, it gets a lot more complicated. Put the gun down and come on out with your hands up."

Matt stayed hunkered down below the window's sightline. He offered no reply for the time being.

"You okay, Murph?" asked Jeff.

Murphy was in the most precarious of positions, sitting square in the middle of two people who were ready to shoot each other. He turned his head to address his friend through the opened window. "I've been meaning to tell you. I joined a book club."

Jeff was confused, but joined in on the conversation, as it would likely distract their assailant. "Really? Have you read anything good?"

"The last book was really long. It had a weird title... it was just some random letters. X... L... V... I... But

Chapter Seven-Seven-Six was really good. Made the entire book worthwhile. I recommend you check it out."

"Chapter Seven-Seven-Six? I actually read that one."

"And?"

"It's one of my favorite chapters," he added, as he fine-tuned his aim towards the car.

Matt was done. In the time it took for them to exchange their book club banter, he came to his ultimate decision. In his mind, there were no options. He knew the abhorrent crimes he committed. He knew exactly what he was guilty of. He knew he was going to jail for a long time, quite probably for the rest of his life. Upon coming to terms with his imminent future, he decided that plan was not acceptable, and it was time to check out. Suicide-by-cop. But if he was leaving this earth, he was most certainly taking someone else with him.

Matt stood up and pointed his gun at Murphy. They locked eyes one last time. "This is all your fault. If I'm going down, so are…"

And before he could complete his sentence, Jeff squeezed off two shots in succession, hitting the aggressor and killing him instantly. The Gunfight on Gulf-to-Bay, as it would later be referred to in police circles, was over.

With the event finally concluded and all parties safe, Jeff turned and finally opened the trunk, and was shocked to discover a bound, gagged and drugged young lady. He and another officer untied her and carried her to the ambulance that just arrived on the scene.

"You're okay," he said, as he gently pulled strands of hair from her face. "You're okay."

He then turned to communicate with a few of the other officers and passed Murphy, still handcuffed in the vehicle.

"I almost shot you, you crazy bastard. How did you know?"

Chapter Sixty-Six

It was a good deed, for sure. With some time to rest and a little therapy, Jordan would recover completely. She now had the rest of her life ahead of her. Murphy's, unfortunately, was still a train wreck. Sure, he would receive some kudos for rescuing an innocent girl, but that didn't change the fact that his career was over, and quite possibly, his freedom, as well. As far as he could see, there wasn't even a glimmer of light at the end of the tunnel. After spending some time giving statements to various officers, it was time to finally head home.

"Your car's wrecked," said Jeff. "We're going to have it towed. Let me take you home."

"Sure"

A million things were racing through his mind. But in the end, all he wanted was a hug from his wife, and assurances they could figure things out. Together.

Murphy and Jeff made some small talk on the way.

"Book club?" asked Jeff.

"I was telling you to take him out."

"Dude, I'm a cop. I know my Florida Statutes. Title XLVI is Crimes, Chapter Seven-Seven-Six is Justifiable Use of Force. Why are you always trying to school me in the law?"

"Just wanted to make sure you knew what had to be done."

"Thanks for the tip. Listen... Seriously... how did you know?"

"Know what?"

"About the girl."

"It's a long story."

"We have time."

"You're gonna laugh."

"Try me."

"I met a psychic..."

"And they told you where she was?"

"Not really, no. But she did say something to me that resonates a lot more now than it did the night she said it."

"What did she say?"

"Psychics claim to have a heightened intuition. She then told me that all people have some sense of intuitive capabilities, some more than others."

"You think you're psychic? Ha! The sleepwalking psychic. That's one I've never heard before," he said with a laugh. "If that were a lounge act in Vegas, I'd buy a ticket."

"I don't think I'm psychic, no, but maybe my intuitive skills, without me even knowing, are above the norm."

"Maybe."

"Sounds a bit more plausible than a ghost told me, doesn't it?"

"Yeah, you really freaked me out with that one."

"I freaked a lot of people out with that one."

Murphy was silent for a moment, and then continued on that same path. "There's something wrong with me, Jeff. My brain seems to be wired differently. I need to figure out why. I think I'm going to take some time off."

"I'm proud of you, man. The first step in solving a problem is admitting you have one."

He debated telling him about being fired and framed for embezzlement, events which were mutually exclusive of each other. But he decided that the person who was most important to him should hear it first. Besides, Jeff was already involved in enough excitement for the day.

"We're here. You want me to come in? Explain to Mollie why you're late?"

"Nah. I'm good."

"Dinner next week?"

"I'd like that."

"I love you, man. But between you and me, I still think you should have let the police do their job."

"From now on, it's all yours. Trust me."

262

Chapter Sixty-Seven

"Babe! I'm home!" he shouted, as he passed through the doorway.

"Hey. Welcome back. I missed you," she replied, and gave him a big hug. "Good trip?"

"Well, it was eventful, that's for sure. Listen... we need to talk."

"Oh, before I forget," she added, "that girl you were worried about... the one from the café... they found her alive. Someone abducted her and had her in their trunk. I just saw it on the news. It was huge. They had to shut down Gulf-to-Bay!"

"Yeah, I heard," he replied, with a half-smile. "Mollie, we really need to talk."

"I agree, but that will need to wait."

"Why is that?"

"We have a visitor."

"Who's here?"

"Come on inside."

Upon turning the corner, he was met with a familiar face.

"Mr. Sterling. Wow, this is... um... quite a surprise."

"Hi Murphy."

"Sir, before you say anything, please let me explain."

"There's nothing to explain," his boss replied.

"Explain what," Mollie asked.

"You got my email?" Murphy asked.

"I did."

Mollie stood there with a surprised look. Something was going on. Something big. But she had no idea.

"Mr. Sterling," he continued, "I am fully prepared to face the music."

"That's good," he replied, "because there are some serious repercussions to this episode."

"I don't understand," quipped Mollie.

"I'll explain later," added Murphy, without breaking eye contact with his boss.

Sterling led the conversation. "Abraham Lincoln once said '*Nearly all men can stand adversity, but if you want to test a man's character, give him power.*'"

Murphy nodded his head, but clearly didn't understand the point he was trying to make. Not yet.

"Part of what made Sterling Investments successful was delegation and autonomy. My goal was always simple: Surround myself with smart people, many of whom were often smarter than me. And then give them the keys to the shop. The intent was to build a team who would run the business like I would. And it worked. It fueled our growth in a very competitive and cutthroat field. But sometimes..." He paused, as he wanted to choose his words carefully. "Sometimes, that plan backfires. I mean, sure, the pond is fully stocked with smart people. But some lack the character necessary to fulfill my vision. Often times I can see it early enough in a person's career. This was not one of those times."

Murphy then knew what he was alluding to. He failed, and he let down the one person who had the most faith in him.

"This is a big mess," concluded Sterling.

"Yes sir. I agree."

"But all is not as it seems, is it?"

"Sir?"

"The truth lies with coffee." To Mollie, it was an odd statement, almost nonsensical. It resembled the random words Murphy would throw together when he was sleepwalking. To Murphy, it was yet another wake-up call, as that was the same exact message he received one night in the pool.

"Sir?" asked Murphy.

"Mollie, would you be so kind and make a pot? I'd love a cup right now. I think it will pave the way and allow us to see things more clearly."

"Umm, sure." Mollie departed for the kitchen, convinced this guy was potentially a few sandwiches short of a picnic.

Murphy was clearly uncomfortable, but forged through the conversation with some small talk so there was no awkward silence. Mollie returned in a matter of minutes with a tray holding three mugs of freshly brewed java. The three sat and sipped.

Sterling inhaled deeply through his nose to get a whiff of the aroma. "Mmmm. Smells great. Earthy aroma." He began stirring his coffee with a cinnamon stick that Mollie had placed on each plate. She had forgotten about Murphy's treatment and post-hypnotic suggestion, but was quickly reminded when her husband leaned in and kissed Sterling on the cheek and said "I love you."

"What the hell is wrong with you?" he shouted.

"Oh, dear God. I am so sorry. It's…" Mollie began to get the giggles and had trouble completing her sentence. "It's a long story."

Sterling took a sip and closed his eyes, as he swished the java through his mouth like a fine wine. "Tastes great, too. Exotic flavor. Pleasant acidity. Tastes fruity, almost citrusy. It reminds me of the Yirgacheffe beans from Ethiopia."

"That's incredible," exclaimed Mollie. "That's exactly what it is. How on earth did you do that?"

"He's a coffee connoisseur. He's got knowledge of beans from all over the world," replied Murphy. "Did you ever get a chance to go into that coffee shop and use the gift card I got you for your birthday?"

Sterling smiled. "I did. Wonderful little coffee bar you stumbled across. I was meaning to ask… how did you find it? It certainly is off the beaten path."

"A friend referred me to it."

"Well, your friend is very smart. They had a spectacular variety of beans available, and I even took a few pounds of exotic grounds home. I prefer the smaller, independent shops over those big coffee chains. It was so much more personal."

He took one more sip and then, inexplicably, poured the rest of the contents of his mug on the floor. Mollie was shocked and reacted as any normal hostess would.

"What the hell are you doing?" She quickly ran into the kitchen to retrieve some paper towels and wipe the mess.

"The truth lies with coffee," he repeated.

"You already said that. I don't…"

Sterling interrupted her before he got himself kicked out of the house. There was a point to that comment, and it was time to make it. "Mollie, look at me. If I asked you for another cup of coffee, would you give me one?"

"No. You're acting crazy and disrespectful in my home."

"You're right. I apologize. But what if it were an accident?"

"That wasn't an accident. You poured it right on the floor."

"I know, but play along for a moment. What if I accidentally bumped into the table and knocked the mug over? You'd still be on the floor, cleaning it up. But would you replace my beverage?"

"I… I guess so."

"While the result, by itself, is something that requires immediate attention, you have to understand the intent before you can make a proper judgment or draw an accurate conclusion."

Murphy and Mollie sat there, dumbfounded and confused. Sterling just smiled.

"As I was saying," Sterling continued with a slight grin on his face, "the independent coffee shops are so much more personal. When I went in for the first time, I met a wonderful young man. He had such a vast knowledge of the beans that were roasted on site. I thought he had been there forever. I mean, it took me years to gain that much insight. You can imagine how shocked I was when he told me he'd only been there for six weeks. I asked what he had done before that, and do you know what he told me?"

The two shook their heads.

"He worked for me. I thought he looked vaguely familiar, but I couldn't place his face. Do you know why he left?"

"No sir."

"He was fired."

"What for?"

"Apparently he found some Accounting irregularities. Associated with your accounts."

Without breaking eye contact, Murphy once again apologized. But Sterling had no interest in listening and charged on. "You sent me an email yesterday, apologizing for your involvement in cheating customers and embezzling money from *my* company."

"You what?!?" screamed Mollie.

Sterling held up one finger. "Hang on... let me finish. You sent me that email, knowing full well that wasn't the truth."

"What is he talking about?"

Murphy was silent.

"Murphy. Goddammit! Look at me. I am your partner in life. What in heaven's name is he talking about?"

"This young man at the coffee shop discovered the irregularities. They were swept under the carpet and he was subsequently let go. And then blackmailed with some risqué photos that were taken during his bachelor party with a couple of escorts, so he wouldn't make any accusations. All, unfortunately, unbeknownst to me."

"Okay, now I'm really confused," said Mollie.

Sterling turned and grabbed the roll of paper towels out of Mollie's hands and finished cleaning the floor. He was a CEO, but he was not beneath kneeling down himself and wiping up the java puddle. "Joe was to be your mentor. But he spilled the coffee on the floor on purpose. He doesn't get any more. Your husband thinks he spilled it, but he didn't. He gets another cup."

He was trying to tell the story using coffee metaphors, but it likely got lost in translation. They were still lost. "Sir?"

"Joe's going to jail, son."

"How did you know it wasn't me?"

"I got a strange email from Lisa in Compliance. She couldn't put her finger on it, but she felt something was amiss. It forced me to do my own, secret investigation."

"And?"

"I don't really like to get involved in people's personal lives... Let's just say I discovered that the first incident took place while you went away for a few days. You weren't even around to execute the crime. A death in the family," he paused as he raised both hands to make air quotes. "I think that was the story you used, was it not?"

Murphy turned his head to Mollie, who smiled, as she slowly recognized that her staged intervention inadvertently provided a solid alibi for a crime she didn't know was committed.

"It, um... it wasn't a death in the family," replied Murphy.

"I know. Amy told me."

"How did she know?" he asked in a surprised tone.

"Who knows how Amy gets her information... For all I know, it was from a friend who has a cousin that's dating someone who repaired the car of someone who was working at the hospital the day you were admitted. All is well, I assume?"

"Yes sir. It was all along."

"I find myself in an unusual situation... unchartered territory, for sure. I was getting ready to promote him to President of Sales, leaving the VP slot vacant until... well... until you were ready. And I see now, more clearly than ever, that you are."

"For VP?"

Sterling smiled. "Close, but no. One notch higher."

"President of Sales? Are you serious?"

"A person's character, Murphy... it's the most important trait, yet it's the hardest to read."

Murphy was elated, but Mollie still felt she was left in the dark. "Hello? Guys, I'm really confused. Can someone please tell me what's going on," she said.

Sterling grabbed Mollie's hands and gave her a short summary, one she undoubtedly deserved. "Your husband had a mentor named Joe. Joe stole some money from the firm. Joe implicated your husband, who had no choice but to keep it under wraps if he wanted to keep his job. But his character wouldn't allow that to happen."

Mollie turned to her husband. "Are you serious? Why didn't you say anything?"

Murphy just shrugged his shoulders. "I couldn't. Mr. Sterling, as excited as I am that you solved this puzzle, I can't help but think..."

"Think what?"

"Well... this is a pretty serious offense. And any way you look at it, it's tied to me."

"Yeah. It's a bit complicated. I'm certain the SEC will want to conduct a full investigation. And I'll probably have to pay a rather large fine. It pains me to do this, but I'm going to have to suspend you. You know, for appearances."

"I understand."

"Let the investigation run its course, and we'll have you back at the firm within the next week or two."

"You sound confident."

"Confidence is what got me where I am today. I wouldn't worry. I've got it all documented. As far as I'm concerned, your name is clear."

"Thank you, sir. This is a huge weight off my shoulders."

"I know. And I'm glad I was able to help right this wrong. By the way, I've also hired back the gentleman at the coffee shop. He'll be reporting to you."

"His name is Robbie, isn't it?" asked Mollie, who finally made sense of cryptic messages that the psychic told her weeks earlier.

"It is," replied Sterling.

"I can't believe I never saw him there," said Murphy. "I've been to that place over a dozen times after work."

"You went after work?"

"Yes, sir."

"Well, that's why. He worked the morning shift. I always went on my way *to* work," replied Sterling.

"Yep. That's it. Well, it'll be an honor working with him, sir. And thank you. For everything."

Chapter Sixty-Eight

Mr. Sterling departed, leaving the two of them dumbfounded at the chain of events that got them to this exact point in time.

"Wow. This is so surreal," commented Mollie.

"You can say that again."

"I can't believe Joe was stealing from the company."

"Yeah, and he did it with my clients... from my computer! I'm sorry I didn't say anything to you, but I didn't know how."

"I understand, now that I know the whole story."

"I'm so glad that's finally over."

"A hell of a journey, but at least there's a silver lining in all of this, Mr. President of Sales."

"Did you ever get my message?" asked Murphy, changing the subject.

"I did, but it cut off at the end."

"I wanted to apologize. About everything."

"You said something about a dream, but you never elaborated."

"I died. In a car accident."

"Oh my God! That's so scary."

"But that wasn't the freaky part. I mean, it was, but…"

"But what?"

"It's hard to put into words."

"Try, baby."

"The accident happened at exactly 2:14am. And I died at 3:57am. That's how I knew!"

"Knew what?"

"Everything! Everything I've been experiencing. My episodes outside. They started and ended at the same time every night!"

"And?" replied Mollie. She wasn't seeing the significance, until Murphy provided clarity.

"That was the time! 2:14am. The vision came at 2:14am every night. And he left at 3:57. Every... Single... Time. It had to be a dream."

"Babe..." she tried to interrupt, but wasn't successful.

"Pablo told me... well, my hallucination stayed exactly an hour and forty-three minutes each time. But I didn't understand the significance. Now I do. In my dream at the hotel, that was the exact amount of time between the accident and the doctor declaring me dead. To the minute! Hon, don't you see? It was all in my mind! Oh, and Joe was speaking Spanish. He called me Pablo."

"He what?"

"He was talking in Spanish. Something about helping his daughter with one of her classes. But he called me Pablo. I had my epiphany right then and there. This crazy, fucked up experience had to be a fabrication developed by my subconsciousness. I somehow weaved this insane... premonition, I guess that's the only way to describe it. It was all in my head."

"A premonition?"

"Yes."

"In your head?"

"Yeah! All of it!"

He was waiting for Mollie to finally exhale after months of worry, and find comfort in this admission. But that wasn't the case.

"Umm…" replied Mollie, who was unsure how to proceed. "I'm not so sure about that."

"What do you mean?"

"I know we talked for months about this, you know, about it being a dream related to your sleepwalking episodes."

"It was. I'm convinced now."

"You had this dream when, three days ago?"

"Yeah."

"I couldn't sleep that night. I mean, that's not unusual. I often have trouble sleeping when you're out of town. It must have something to do with me being alone in a cavernous king-sized bed. But this time it seemed different. I don't know why. I was exhausted the next morning, and started the day with a larger-than-average cup of coffee to wake me up. I grabbed a magazine and went to sit outside by the pool and saw…"

"What did you see?"

"I saw three used cigarettes in an ash tray."

"You saw what? That's impossible!"

"I know, it's crazy. Every day you told me Pablo would smoke three cigarettes when he visited. I always thought it was you."

"It had to be me," he answered confidently.

"Please, let me finish. I convinced myself that's how you released your stress. And while it kind of freaked me out that you started smoking, I rationalized it because it was such a small number. But this time… There was nobody here but me. You were away on business."

"That is freaky."

"Yeah..." she said, clearly inferring there was more to this story. "You should sit down for this next part."

Murphy glanced at her with a perplexed look, but followed her instruction like a trained pet as he waited for the next words to come out of her mouth.

"I called Mel."

"Melissa? Why?"

"I asked her to see if she could pull any DNA or fingerprints off the cigarette butts."

"And?"

"DNA takes too long. But she did find prints."

"And?"

There was a moment of silence before Mollie shared the inexplicable. "They belong to a man named Benjamin Adler."

"What?! Are you serious? Someone snuck onto our property?"

"Honey..."

"Did you call the police?"

"Babe... Benjamin Adler is dead. He died eighteen years ago."

Murphy was silent. He tried desperately to make sense of this, but there was literally no way to process this new information.

"So... I researched him online, you know, to find out whatever I could about him. He died in a car accident while on a business trip. He had a wife named Joanne and a daughter who was born after he died. Her name was..."

And before Mollie could complete her sentence, Murphy finished it for her. "Jordan."

"Yeah. Jordan. How... how did you know that?"

Murphy didn't reply, instead he just repeated his last statement. "He had a daughter... named Jordan." And then it hit her.

"Wait... the girl at the coffee shop. The one I just saw on the news? Wasn't that her name?"

He nodded in reply.

"That's an odd coincidence, don't you think?"

"It's not a coincidence," Murphy replied, nonchalantly.

"What do you mean it's not a... Wait! What are you saying? Are you telling me...?"

Murphy just nodded.

"That's his daughter? Oh my God, I have goose bumps."

"Hang on," he replied. "Don't talk. I need a minute or two to process this."

Murphy and his wife sat silently, allowing the situation to be absorbed.

"It all makes sense now," he began.

"Are you serious? None of this makes sense."

"So, Pablo was real?"

"I... have no choice but to agree with you. I'm so sorry I doubted you."

"Don't beat yourself up over it. I would've done the same thing and institutionalized you if you told me that story."

Mollie smiled. "I guess there are just some things in the world that we can't explain."

"Everything I encountered... actually happened. We had a ghost in our pool."

"It looks that way. I'm just sorry I never had a chance to meet him. He only came around when you were alone."

"Yeah, he wanted to meet you, but he told me he never had any control of his comings and goings. He...wait... You said he was here the other night."

"Right."

"While I was away."

"Which was odd for him, wouldn't you say, given his pattern?"

"No. Jesus, no. I know why he came. He knew I was gone. He didn't come to see me. He came to see you."

"What?"

"Our first night in the pool... I only agreed to go in if he promised to visit you. I told him the only way I could convince you he was real is if he physically met you. He promised he would before he..." Murphy stopped before completing his sentence.

"Before he what?"

"Passed over to the other side."

"What does that mean?"

"Eternal peace. It was his final journey. He came to see *you* because he... well, he must have known I would complete the task that was assigned to him."

"What task was that?"

"He had to save a random soul."

"Sounds like it wasn't that random."

"He didn't know. Every day he told me he had to intervene and help someone. I'll bet my life he had no idea the person he had to help was his daughter. In fact, he didn't know who he was supposed to help until a few days ago."

"So, that whole thing on the news? That was him?"

"Actually... he had a 'Field of Dreams' thing going on. He couldn't leave our property."

"What are you saying?"

277

"He made me his ambassador."

"Wait! Everything I saw on the news... the closing of Gulf-to-Bay in all directions... crashed cars, police with guns drawn... that was you? That's why you were late tonight?"

"Guilty as charged."

"And you're sure he didn't know the person he needed to help was his daughter?"

"I'm positive."

"Well, if he didn't know, then how...?"

"I can't believe I'm saying this, but the universe knew. Apparently, that's what brought us together. I guess now he can pass on, pass through, pass over, whatever it was he said he couldn't do."

The two were quiet for a few moments, absorbing all the details.

"I wonder why he called himself Pablo if his name was Benjamin?" he asked.

Mollie grabbed his hand. "It's in his eulogy that I found online. It was a nickname they gave him at work, and it just stuck."

"He owned a restaurant."

"Yeah. How did you know?"

Murphy smiled. "He's the one who gave me those new recipes I've been trying out on you."

"No way!"

"Yeah. We've spent quite a few nights together. We learned a lot about each other. I really feel like I know him quite well."

"You hung out with him for three months and now you're best friends?"

"The length of the friendship doesn't dictate the strength of the friendship. I just can't believe it...

Everything he told me, everything he showed me… it was all true."

Mollie smiled. "You're a good man, Murphy. Come here and give me a hug."

Murphy got off the couch and approached his bride. He placed his arms around her and pulled her closely towards him.

"Ow!"

"What's the matter, baby?"

"Something under your shirt just jabbed me."

"Oh… it's just my necklace."

Mollie unbuttoned part of her top to expose her jewelry. It wasn't new, but it was new to him.

"What's that?"

"A pendant."

"That pendant looks familiar."

"That's impossible. I've never worn it before. I was saving it for a very special occasion." And as soon as those words come out of her mouth, she became emotional.

"I swear that pendant looks familiar… it looks just like… wait a minute." And then it clicked.

Murphy held the pendant in his hands. It was a Chinese symbol, identical to the tattoo Jordan had on her wrist. The universe was full of signs, and he was now more susceptible to seeing them. He knew what the symbol meant, and why she was crying. And he knew what her next words were going to be. But he had to ask. He wanted to hear it come out of her mouth. He *needed* to hear it come out of her mouth.

"There's a personal meaning to this pendant, isn't there?"

Mollie nodded, with a few additional tears streaming down her face. She became so emotional she could barely say the words. "We're pregnant."

"Oh my God. I knew you were going to say that! I just knew it!"

"And it's a girl."

"Really? Wow... I'm gonna be a dad... to a little girl."

"I love you," she said. "Thank you so much."

"For what? Making a baby was a team effort."

She then whispered in his ear. "For not getting in that car."

The two could barely hold back the tears, and hugged silently for what seemed like an eternity.

Chapter Sixty-Nine

"Come to bed with me, baby," she said, as she reached out to hold his hand.

"I will. In a few minutes."

"You're staying up?"

"Just a few minutes. I'm still trying to process all of this."

Mollie smiled. "Okay, but don't take too long. You need your rest. And no more swimming with ghosts, okay?"

Murphy grinned back at her. "I think that chapter's finally over."

Mollie departed towards the bedroom, leaving him in the kitchen. He opened the sliding glass door and walked outside onto the lanai. He sat down at the pool's edge with his feet dangling in the water and began staring at the shallow end.

"Let me see if I got this straight," he began. "You were stuck in ghost jail and the only way to get out was to help an innocent teen navigate the most difficult chapter of her life. A beautiful young lady who grew up without a father because he died in a car accident before she was born. You then, somehow, figured out a way to fuck with me so that I was able to avoid getting into a car that I dreamed would crash, allowing me to be here, today. Here. Today.

To hear my wife tell me that we are finally pregnant. With a girl. A girl who can now grow up with a father, because you taught me how to read the signs. If I didn't know all the details, I'd say you *were* playing a scene from Dickens. But it was more than that, wasn't it? Your baby was in trouble. The universe knew she would face a violent chapter in her life when she was eighteen. That's why you couldn't pass over. They kept you in limbo until she was safe. They needed your help. And you needed mine."

Murphy paused, awaiting an answer he knew would never come.

"I was assaulted, arrested, and committed to a psychiatric facility. Oh yeah, and I wrecked my car. All because of you. I'm still trying to wrap my mind around all of this, but… thank you."

He stood up and walked towards the house to head back inside and join his bride. The sliding glass door was barely open when he heard three random bubbles surface from the bottom of the pool. *Pop, pop, pop.* It was probably just some air working its way through the filter system. But based on the recent chain of events, he couldn't help but think… maybe it was a message… a reply of three simple syllables. *'No…thank you.'*

He stared, once again, at the pool. Instead of going inside, he walked to the other side of the lanai. He then pulled out a half-pack of cigarettes that were hidden in the barbecue grill, and gently placed them on the patio table. "Something tells me you won't be coming by anymore, but I'll leave these here just in case you do." He held his hand up and waved goodbye. "Enjoy the journey. God speed, Pablo."

Gregg Winston

Chapter Seventy

The following week at the café.

"Well, look who it is. Can't get enough of me, can you?"

"Don't flatter yourself, Shorty. I'm just here for the coffee. Can I get two cups of your favorite blend?"

"Skim milk?"

Murphy smiled. "Cream, please."

"Sure. And who is your beautiful companion?"

"Jordan, I'd like you to meet my wife, Mollie. Mollie, this is Jordan."

"So, this is Jordan," she said, with her hand outreached for a handshake. "It's a pleasure to finally meet you."

"Same here," she replied, as she grabbed her hand. "Murphy has told me so much about you."

"We've had one hell of a ride, haven't we?" he asked.

"You can say that again."

Mollie placed her hand on her husband's shoulder. "Hon, I'm going to get a seat and give you two a chance to catch up."

"Okay. I'll bring your cup once it's brewed."

Jordan and Murphy continued with their small talk, until a stranger interrupted. "You're not going to introduce me?"

"Sorry," replied Jordan. "Murphy, this is my mom, Abby."

283

"Your mom? Wow, what an honor. It's an absolute pleasure to meet you."

Murphy knew she was special. If what happened *really happened*, that made her Pablo's wife, and this chance encounter made the afternoon that much more special. Deep down, he wanted to say something. He wanted to share the bizarre, yet fulfilling journey he took... the whole thing. But he knew he couldn't. The story was just too unbelievable.

"Oh, no. Truly, the honor is mine. Thank you so much for everything. She's my whole world."

"I'm just glad it all worked out."

"Me too. Was that your wife who just sat down?"

"It was."

"Do you mind if I grab a seat and say hi? I'd love to sit and chat with you both, if you have the time."

"No, not at all. I'll be over in a minute."

Abby departed and introduced herself to Mollie. Though nobody knew each other, they all quickly became friends, as they were linked through an inexplicable chain of events.

"Do you live around here?" asked Abby.

"Us? No. We're about forty minutes away. Over in Clearwater. Why do you ask?"

"Oh. It's just... your husband looks familiar. I just can't seem to recall from where."

"He has come here quite frequently. It's been a regular stop for him lately."

"No... that's not it. Well, I'm sure it'll come to me."

"Your daughter is beautiful."

"Thank you. I'm so thrilled everything worked out. When she first went missing, my whole world fell apart. I

284

completely freaked out. But your husband seemed to have it all under control."

"It might look that way, but deep down, he was a mess. We all were. Everything that happened... it affected us all." She, too, wanted to say something, as she was as much a part of the journey as he was. In the end, however, she came to the same decision as her spouse. There's no way that story could be told without somebody thinking they were a family of lunatics.

Murphy approached with his two cups of java and sat next to his wife, facing Jordan's mom.

"When I first met Jordan and realized what an extraordinary young lady she was," he began, "I said to myself, I'd really like to meet her parents. I'm glad we came down here today. What are the odds you were going to be here? I guess this is fate."

"I'm the only parent. Her father died before she was born. I never remarried. He would be so proud to see what a beautiful young lady she has become," commented Abby.

Mollie grabbed Murphy's hand. "It must have been hard, you know, raising her by yourself."

"It was. Thankfully, we..." Abby stopped in mid-sentence and started staring at Murphy.

"Is... everything okay?"

Abby offered no reply, she just continued looking deeply into his eyes, as if she was connecting with his soul.

"Abby?"

"I knew I recognized you!"

"I'm sorry?"

"From the moment I laid eyes on you."

"Did we work together?"

285

"No, sir."

"Did you sit in on one of my seminars?"

"No sir."

"I didn't invest money for you? That's what I do. I'm a financial advisor, of sorts."

"No," she answered with a smile.

"Why are you smiling," asked Mollie.

"This is just ironic. I mean, really ironic."

"You've piqued my curiosity. Besides, these days, irony is my middle name. Where did we meet?"

"We met a long time ago. It was a week after my husband died. I had family over. The life insurance company sent someone over to deliver a check."

"Wait…"

"You came in, saw that I was ready to give birth, and ran to the bathroom and threw up."

Mollie's eyes grew as big as saucers. She knew this story, as she had heard it a hundred times before. But it was always he who told it.

"That couldn't possibly have been you. I've only delivered one check in my life, and I quit right after that."

"You don't remember?"

"I remember everything about that day."

"But you don't remember me?"

"You look much different than I remembered."

"We cried together."

"I cried like a baby," replied Murphy. "It was… it was so emotional. I was never that close to death before. Are you serious? That was you?"

"You wanted to leave so fast, but you kept tripping over the furniture, knocking over all the drinks. Then you got lightheaded and had to sit down."

Murphy looked at Mollie in amazement. What the hell were the odds their paths would cross again, almost two decades later. She shrugged her shoulders, as if to say "this is no crazier than what we've been through."

"Do you remember what you said to me?"

"I don't. I honestly don't. I was so young. Not only that… delivering that check, it just freaked me out. I was a mess."

"I tried to calm you down. I grabbed your hand and put it on my stomach. You felt the baby… Jordan… you felt Jordan kick."

"Her?" he asked incredulously, as he pointed to the young lady behind the cash register at the front of the café. "I felt her kick?"

"Yeah."

"Almost two decades ago?"

"Ironic, right?"

"Holy crap. You think I freaked out then, that's got nothing on how I feel right now," he added.

"You tried to offer me comfort. You apologized for my loss, and said although my husband was gone, you were certain he would protect her from up above, you know, from heaven. And then you said if he needed any help… this was so funny… if he needed any help, he could just come down and ask you for assistance. All you needed was a sign."

Mollie was dumbfounded, her jaw practically dropped to the floor. "You said that?"

"Maybe. I mean, I don't remember."

"Oh, I remember," replied Abby. "Yes, you said that. I might have a few of the words wrong, but that was your sentiment. I guess it's safe to say you got some sort of sign, because my baby is safe, thanks to you."

Murphy looked at Mollie and raised one eyebrow, telepathically asking her, "should we tell her?" Mollie replied with a smile and an ever-so-gentle shake of her head.

"I guess I did," he replied, as his attention turned back to his new friend. "The universe is quite vocal when it wants to be."

Chapter Seventy-One

Two weeks had come and gone quickly. Murphy spent most of it working on the nursery. Sure, having a baby was still months away, but there was plenty to do, and he was thrilled to finally be doing it. Today was the start of a new week, but this one was extra special. His investigation was fast-tracked, his name cleared, and he was ready to head back to work.

"Stay still."

"I'm trying. I'm just nervous."

"I know, but if you don't stop moving around, I'll never get this tied."

"I'm a little surprised."

"At what," she said, as she tried tying it for the third time.

"I think this is the first time you're not referring to it as a silly bowtie."

"Let's just say I'm a little more inclined these days to believe in luck and superstition. There. Done. Looks great."

Murphy turned around to look in the living room mirror.

"Dang. I must say, you've got skills."

"Oh, you have no idea, mister."

"I think I'm ready."

Swimming with Ghosts

"I think you are, too. What's first on the agenda today?"

"Meeting with the team. And since I'm at the top of the food chain, it's a pretty big team."

"You should leave now and try to get there early. You don't want to make a bad first impression and show up late."

"Yeah, you're right. Well… I'm off. Wish me luck."

"Trust me, lover. You don't need luck. Just do me one favor, please."

"What's that?"

"Now that you're in charge, you get to make some big decisions, right?"

"Right," he answered, not sure where she was going with this.

"I need you to ban cinnamon sticks in the break room."

"That's a weird request. They're going to think I'm crazy right out of the gate."

"Trust me."

"Got it. No cinnamon sticks. Any other last words of advice?"

"Nope. Just be yourself."

"Thanks, baby."

And with that final comment, he left the house to begin a drive that he had done a thousand times before, yet this time, it felt a little different. He began his commute by syncing his phone to the car stereo so he could listen to his "road trip" playlist. Ten minutes into the drive, while singing along to "For Those About to Rock, We Salute You" by AC/DC, he noticed a stranded car on the side of the road. Standing next to the car was a young girl. He was in a rush to get to work and address the forty or so people who now reported to him, but as he passed her, the

290

thought of Pablo raced through his mind. If there was anything he learned about his recent experiences, it's that everyone is in their own world, and at some point, we all need help. He remembered his drives with Joe, who clearly wouldn't lend assistance even if he had the time. If nothing else, Murphy learned that karma was a real thing, and any good deed would most certainly pay dividends down the road. Though he didn't have the time to help her, he decided to anyway. He pulled his car onto the right shoulder, and put the car in reverse so he could safely back up and get closer to this random soul who needed a friend.

"Looks like someone could use a hand," he said to the stranded stranger.

With a despondent look on her face, she replied "I need more than a hand. I need a miracle. I called for a tow truck, but the auto club said this is their busiest time of the day, and it would take two hours for someone to show up."

"Well then, it's a good thing I stopped by. What seems to be the problem?"

"Passenger side, rear tire is flat. Thank you so much for stopping. I'm freaking out because today is my first day on a new job. When I was hired, they told me the most important thing was punctuality. And now I'm going to be late. On my first day! I'm going to be fired as soon as I get there, I know it."

"Take a deep breath. I know how nerve-wracking it can be. It's actually my first day on a new job, too."

"Are you serious? Well, now I feel awful. I don't want to make you late on your first day."

"It's all good. How about we tackle this together? I'm certain we can get you on your way quickly if we join forces."

"Thank you. I'm so grateful. If there was ever a day that I needed a guardian angel, it's today."

Murphy smiled, took off his blazer and rolled up his sleeves. "Okay, let's get the spare out of your trunk."

She leaned in the driver side of the car and popped the trunk. He made some small talk as he pulled out the spare, in an effort to ease her frame of mind. "How far away is the office?"

"From here? Only about fifteen, maybe twenty minutes."

"Okay... you'll be late, but not too late."

"Yeah, but they said..."

"Are you a hard worker?"

"Yes sir!"

"Are you dependable?"

"There's nobody more dependable than me."

"Then they will be thrilled to have you on their team."

A stranger's words did little to put her at ease.

"You're nervous, aren't you?"

"Terrified."

"Look... you're gonna be late. It is what it is. Own it. There's nothing you can do to change that. Admit to it and then give them your elevator speech."

"My what?"

"Here's what I think you should do. You need to walk in there and announce your presence."

"Announce my presence?"

"Yes. What's your name?"

"Erica. Erica Ross."

"You should walk in there, confidently, and say 'My name is Erica Ross. Today is my first day, and I'm late. But I'm here today to give you everything I've got, and to help this company be all it can be.'"

"Do you think that's a good idea? Calling attention to my tardiness?"

"Does it make you uncomfortable?"

"Yes."

"I had a good friend who once offered me some wise advice. He said to do the things that make you uncomfortable. That's what builds character."

"If you say so. Oh my God," she exclaimed, as she pointed to his shirt. "The tire left a huge mark on you."

"It's okay."

"I am so sorry."

"It's okay."

"But you said it's your first day, too. And I ruined your shirt."

"I believe today is going to be a great first day. For both of us."

Murphy finished changing the tire and tightened every lug, one at a time. "You, my new friend, are good to go."

"Thank you."

"Good luck today. You're going to do great."

"Thank you. I hope you have a great day, as well."

Murphy grabbed his blazer, threw it in the car and sped off. Erica pulled herself together and drove well within the speed limit, taking his advice. "When I get there, I get there."

She pulled into the parking lot and walked towards the building. She paused at the employee entrance and took a deep breath. As she walked in, she saw a group of people huddled at a stand-up meeting. She had received advice from a random stranger who helped her navigate a difficult morning. She felt the stars were aligned and trusted him. She was going to do what he said. She approached the crowd and cleared her throat.

"Hello?"

The crowd became quiet and all at the same time turned to look at her.

"Own it," she said to herself. "Do what makes you uncomfortable." And she did. "Hi. My name is Erica Ross. Today is my first day, and I'm late. But I'm here today to give you everything I've got, and to help this company be all it can be."

The person in charge took a few steps and parted the group of people like Moses in the Dead Sea, so he or she could get a better look at this person who interrupted their meeting with her tardiness. Life was all about first impressions. She was certainly taking a gamble with this one. Her fear turned to relief once she locked eyes on their leader, a man with a dirty shirt who stopped to help a stranger change a flat tire, on the first day of *his* new job.

"Ms. Ross," he shouted. "You're late."

"Yes sir. I am," she answered confidently.

The two of them exchanged smiles. The group was silent, until Murphy replied loudly for all to hear. "Welcome to Sterling Investments, Ms. Ross. We're thrilled to have you on our team. Please, come on over and join us."